GODS PLAYGROUND

∞

CHERYL SKORY SUMA

EXCEPTIONALITIES MEDIA, TORONTO, CANADA

gods Playground © 2019
Date of First Publication: Jan 2019

All other works herin including the cover and layout © 2019 Exceptionalities Media Inc

ISBN 978-0-9939591-4-1

Other Versions:
Ebook ISBN 978-0-9939591-5-8

Published by:
EXCEPTIONALITIES MEDIA
Toronto, Canada
www.ExceptionalitiesMedia.com

CONTENTS

PROLOGUE

As part of my punishment, I must lay out this account. My memory is flawless, and I am all out of lies.

So pull up your figurative chair, and listen to what I did. Then you can judge if I rose to the occasion or if I'm the fallen hero, the failed protagonist. Perhaps you'll even despise me.

Either way, your opinion and conclusions mean nothing to me. Yet I will tell you anyway, as all that I have left now is the telling.

I am god Number 201. This is your and my story.

One
PUPPET MASTER

The dank warehouse smelled of exhaust fumes and wet cardboard. I darted agilely between the rows of forgotten things, looking for somewhere to hide. My borrowed heart was pounding fiercely and the lungs of the body I had Possessed felt as though they were collapsing.

If I keep this up, I'm going to kill him.

The idea was exciting. I had never experienced death while within a Host body before, and I couldn't help but wonder what it would feel like.

"You've nowhere else to run, Constantine," my Host's nemesis said from behind me.

Gasping, my back still turned, I did my best to sound afraid.

"This is true. Perhaps you win after all, Marcus."

My body's lack of breath and its permeating exhaustion helped add depth to my faux terror, but I was secretly thrilled by the exhilaration of this final confrontation. I turned to face him.

Marcus held a gun clutched tightly between his two outstretched hands. He hesitated; I saw his arms sink. Was he wise to me? Impossible. I had played my part too well.

"Prepare to meet your maker!"

I suppressed a laugh. He sounded like a mobster from an old black and white movie.

"Yes, the Maker," I mumbled, immediately realizing how unafraid I sounded.

"I mean… I'm not afraid to die. You'll pay for this, Marcus. My men will seek revenge for my death!"

I peered anxiously into his eyes, hoping that he bought my nervousness as genuine fear of my impending demise.

Marcus raised his weapon back in line with my chest. Yet again, he paused.

"Constantine, you…." He shook his head. "You must pay for what you've done." Marcus frowned.

I began to panic. The rules of vacationing in gods Playground are very clear. Very precise. Very unbreakable. *Become the Host. Act as he would act. Choose as he would choose. Be human. The Host, and all humans around the Host, must never realize that the Host is Possessed.*

"Please, Marcus, have mercy! Spare my life; I will do anything you want!" I must sound terrified for the life that I was only borrowing.

"Shut up!" he barked.

Now he will shoot me, I thought with relief.

I was enjoying this latest Vacation experience so much that time seemed to go in slow motion. I watched with unsuppressed fascination as the bullet left the gun to travel like a floating pearl across the warehouse floor towards my chest.

Remarkable! Not at all what I expected!

I couldn't help but be surprised by the sensation of the bullet entering the flesh. At first, it felt no different than the pressure of someone touching your arm. Like the touch of a lover.

The next instant was less interesting and much less romantic. Quite uncomfortable, actually.

It felt as though I was being ripped apart from the inside, as my flesh recoiled into itself. A searing bright pain, blinding and all-consuming in its glory, flashed through my chest. I collapsed to the ground, surprised to feel the jolt of the cement floor on my knees even through the fire exploding in my ribcage.

Then Constantine's own consciousness flashed to the surface, catching me off guard, and I began to lose the connection. To my surprise, I experienced a twinge of unfamiliar guilt.

Following this extraordinary brightness of being, everything went dark. As my surroundings began to glow, I looked around me.

Shit, I'm home.

I moved through the clustered lights, down the path my kind knew all too well. Time to give my Vacation Satisfaction Report.

I paused. I selfishly wanted to relish in the short-term memories, to reminisce about Constantine.

I hope you won't be missed, I thought, then immediately chided myself for the sentiment. Was there no end to my aberrant responses today?

I reached the check-in counter.

"A pleasant trip, we hope?" the Controller asked agreeably.

"Yes, quite. I experienced my first death."

"Oh, how exciting for you! Was it a car crash, a fire?"

I shook my head.

"Perhaps a drowning, heart attack?"

Observing my blank expression, she speculated enthusiastically, "No, a murder!" She smiled self-satisfactorily when I nodded.

"Were you stabbed?"

"Shot, actually."

"Fabulous! Did you feel the flash? The moment of death's reclaiming of the Host? The onset of eternity?" She smiled again, then looked back down at her record to make a notation.

I shifted uncomfortably, not sure what to reveal, not sure what I felt.

"Sort of, yes. It wasn't quite what I'd expected."

She raised her eyes from her notes.

"You know, he was going to die anyway; it was already going to happen. You didn't change his future. You were a respectful guest of gods Playground."

Shrugging off my misgivings, I couldn't quite decide why I felt so unsettled. For starters, I knew she was lying. We gods frequently influenced and changed our Hosts' futures. Fate is a fable that the Controllers offer to appease any guilt that may arise from vacationers. All gods know this yet pretend otherwise.

"Do you think I could go back right away?" I surprised myself with the question.

"Ha! Then your Vacation *was* a success."

Leaning closer, she whispered, "I'm supposed to get a full debrief, then have you complete a new Vacation Application Request before you go back. However, I've been known to make an exception…."

Looking around and seeing no other guests, she smiled conspiratorially.

"You want to see the funeral, don't you? You want to see which Earthbounds come to mourn, to see what happens after the end?"

Actually, I hadn't been thinking anything of the sort, but as soon as she said it, I realized that I did want to go to the funeral. For what reason, I can honestly say, I had none. Other than, I suppose, I felt like I should. It was my first death, after all.

"Could you help me do that? Just a quick look."

"Let's see." She peered into her Controller's Overseer display, its screen lighting up her wide smile. She seemed to be enjoying this break from protocol.

"Time is a-tickin', earth time is a-flowin'. If I can just lock into the funeral timeline, I might…." She hunched even closer to the busy display, fingers flying as she scrolled rapidly through multiple profiles.

She sat back up, beaming. She waved at the screen. "Got it! Who do you want, the estranged father? The girlfriend? There's his closest mafia business partner… oh wait, what about his grade-school friend? No one at the funeral knows him well. He should be an easy one to play convincingly on such short notice."

"Sure, yes, I'll take the friend."

I was anxious to go back before she changed her mind. Before she decided to make me wait, had m fill out the Vacation Application after all — or decided that the overlap in lifelines was too risky and insisted I select a new Vacation map.

"The grade-school chum it is, then. Don't forget the Memory Upload. I'll place you just as he arrives at the funeral. He's driving there now."

She tapped her pen on the Overseer display. "Oh, you should note that his profile says he's very bright, disciplined, but a bit reserved. He's also got an odd mark on his file, destined for some future greatness, apparently. Perhaps you'll witness his rise to glory."

I wished she'd stop speaking and just send me. The feeling of urgency was growing.

"Hey! Hold up. Don't you want to know your name? It's Adam. Adam Juri."

She apparently needed to be humored in exchange for her orchestration of my expedited return to the Playground.

"Jury, like judge and jury? That's funny," I responded with false lightheartedness.

"No, Juri like the Slavic word that means farmer. See you soon! Please represent Adam well, and be a good guest of gods Playground. Don't do anything I wouldn't do."

With a small chuckle and a shake of her head, she waved me off, her dalliance with me already forgotten.

*   *   *

The first moment you enter a Host is the worst.

The best way I can describe it is that it's like putting on someone else's dirty shoes. It just feels wrong, repulsive.

Then their consciousness goes to sleep, and you start to feel more like yourself. It quickly gets better after that.

As I entered Adam, he flinched, causing his hands to slip from the wheel. The sedan swerved sharply right, and I was barely able to pull the car back in time to avoid Adam upending us in the ditch along the cemetery driveway.

I pulled the vehicle to a screeching stop on the soft shoulder. Several men and women dressed in black looked back towards the sound, then whispered to their neighbors.

Way to make an entrance, Adam, I chided him/myself.

Looking down, I could see that I was wearing a dark suit. Expensive looking, with a sharp tie and equally spotless, polished shoes. Flipping down the visor, I was pleased to see that despite my Host's careful attire, I was, at least, on the more rugged side of handsome.

"Well, Adam, best join the crowd and exchange pleasantries." I snickered to myself, knowing full well that Adam as anyone knew him was long gone.

Gone until I decided to leave him.

As I approached the assembly of mourners, I worked myself into character. Adam's Memory Upload had indicated that he and Constantine had been inseparable as children and had remained very close friends into adulthood despite their different choices. Adam came from a well-to-do family. Constantine's family lottery had not been so lucky.

They had bonded at school over their shared sense of humor and inquisitive natures. Adam had pursued higher education, his entrepreneurial personality eventually leading him to found his own advertising business. Constantine, meanwhile, had quickly gone astray after losing touch with his stable friend. He fell in with the wrong crowd, eventually choosing to embrace a life of crime and violence within the American mafia, consumed with the pursuit of easy money and power.

As adults, they have drifted apart, and Adam had not spoken to Constantine in years. Strangely, Adam's Memory Upload did not indicate why he'd chosen to attend the funeral or even how he knew that Constantine had died.

The group of mourners was huddled together in an awkward clump beside the casket. The priest was rambling on about the sorrow of death, the sadness of a life wasted by crime. Several of the attendees were crying while others stood stoically, waiting for the service to end.

As I stepped up to join the fringe of the group, I stumbled slightly as I recognized Marcus.

What a surprise to see him here!

His eyes were less crazed than the last time I'd seen them over the barrel of his gun, but his presence was still menacing to me.

Obviously, no one here knew that he had murdered Constantine.

He was standing in the middle of the gathering, nodding sympathetically in rhythm with the priest's speech, his left arm draped comfortingly across the shoulder of a petite woman in a burgundy coat.

How deliciously evil that he would choose to attend. I'd found a new respect for Marcus. Such bravado! What a treat — to look into the eyes of your own murderer after the fact.

Then, too late, I realized my error and tried to avert my eyes. But it was no use; he'd spotted me.

I gave a weak smile. His brow furrowed as he locked his gaze with mine.

There it was, inescapable and clear. The crux of the problem. The main reason we are generally not permitted to return and possess relatives or friends of past Hosts.

It can be summed up very simply by the old human adage, "the eyes are the true mirror to the soul." Despite a new skin, when we encounter past Earthbound acquaintances, we gods can still stir up feelings of familiarity. A sense of recognition. Yet here I was, dipping back into the same pool.

I prayed he would dismiss the feeling of recognition that I inspired.

Thankfully, Marcus broke our connection, then leaned down to whisper something into the ear of the woman he had clutched under his arm. She pulled away, seemingly disturbed rather than comforted. She then lifted her head and spotted my arrival.

Uhh….

I realized that I had gasped out loud.

Her eyes were a deep emerald green, large and piercing, framed by dark lashes. Red from crying, they still demanded your consideration.

Even in her apparent sorrow, her face was striking, with high cheekbones and full lips. Her perfect features were framed by long, thick, amber hair that seemed to flow about her face despite the lack of a breeze — or more likely, I'd watched too many romance movies while Earthbound. Either way, beyond her physical attractiveness, it was the depth in her eyes that now pulled me in.

The priest concluded and the crowd began to dissipate. Stepping away from Marcus, the woman who had captured my attention extended her hand.

"Thank you for coming."

Her voice was as deep and sensual as I had already imagined it would be.

"Yes, of course. I'm Adam," I sputtered, shocked by my own visceral reaction.

"Adam…."

The sound of my new name on her lips was like honey, like a symphony. My head spun. What kind of god was I, to be so shaken by this Earthbound?

She smiled, waiting for me to explain myself.

"Sorry, of course, you don't know me. I'm Adam Juri, Constantine's school chum."

As the priest walked away and the stragglers scattered, Marcus cast one last suspicious glare at me then walked off as well.

The vision, meanwhile, let loose a wholehearted laugh. This should have seemed horribly out of place at a funeral, but somehow, coming for her, it felt completely natural.

"Chum? What are you, British? I don't detect an accent."

Leaning closer until the smell of her perfume surrounded me, she peered into my eyes.

"I didn't know that Constantine kept in touch with any old friends from his childhood. He never spoke of you."

I was not handling this Possession very well. She had completely thrown me off. I'd only meant to observe — I hadn't planned to talk to anyone.

"And you are?" I hoped to divert her attention away from my poor performance.

Crinkling her eyes, her lips twitched in an endearing cross between puzzlement and amusement.

"Evangeline. I'm the widow, of sorts."

She glanced around. Seeing that the other visitors had all left, she added sharply, "I don't know which Constantine you knew as a child, but the one I knew was a lousy boyfriend. Kind of an asshole recently, actually. I was considering calling the whole thing off, hadn't spoken to him in over a week before he was killed. He had this habit of disappearing lately…." She looked back at the casket.

A sigh. "I should have left him long ago."

Taken aback by her honesty, I froze. I had lived Constantine's life for several days before he died, and I agreed. He was a horrible person, a man fallen from grace.

However, I, as Adam, shouldn't know this. I was supposed to be his grief torn friend. I should be outraged by her casual dismissal of his life.

How had I missed that he had a girlfriend? If I hadn't let him die, we would have met under better circumstances.

She'd already have a thing for me.

"I don't know who he became after we lost touch, but he was my best friend growing up. Funny, witty, loyal. When I heard he'd died, I had to come."

I tried to look stern when all I really wanted to do was kiss her. *Damn you, dead Constantine! Couldn't you have thought of her once last week?* Perhaps the Controller had decided Evangeline wasn't relevant to my Vacation. Controllers did love to keep creative control.

Evangeline sighed, then ran her hand across her forehead and through her hair, as though pulling away unwanted thoughts.

"He didn't die. He was murdered by one of his mafia associates. He's gone because he was a criminal. Because he hung out with criminals."

She began to walk across the cemetery. I obligingly fell in step beside her, determined to prolong our exchange as long as possible.

Turning her mesmerizing face back towards me, she said cheekily, "Maybe you should take me to lunch, Mr. Juri. So you can tell me about the *good* Constantine. The boy I never knew. I would like to think of him fondly, rather than be glad to be free of him."

I wondered what her parents looked like, what she had been like as a child. I wondered if she found Adam attractive.

Misinterpreting my lack of response to mean I required more convincing, she turned her face back up towards me, her moon eyes sparkling.

"Plus, no one else here cares about me. Maybe you could — since we have our sick, unrequited love for Constantine in common."

I was in over my head. My borrowed gut screamed that I should leave before I slipped up and revealed knowledge I had received while living as Constantine. Knowledge that Adam shouldn't have.

This was the exact reason Controllers normally frowned upon gods returning to the same stomping ground of a past Host. Overlapping lifelines were too risky. I wondered again why the Controller had allowed me to return.

"I would be delighted." I gestured toward my car. "Do you know a nice place? I just arrived from Chicago. I'm afraid I don't know New York very well."

"I know just the place."

Surprising me once again, she reached out and laced her arm through my own. Feeling like a king, I walked her to Adam's car.

I was hooked.

* * *

Following a series of convoluted directions, we arrived at her chosen destination. I drove the sedan into an empty parking spot in front. The building's façade was simple and suggested the weariness of a place that had a cult following but no longer cares for new customers.

"This is where you want to go for lunch?"

She shrugged. "I'll have more fun if you're uncomfortable, stuffy-pants." Cocking her head to one side, she pulled on my arm. "Come on, I'll introduce you."

What is wrong with me? I had a feeling Adam would never have gone to lunch with her, at least not here. I still had the advantage of being the mystery friend. I'd pulled off more challenging Possessions before; I just needed to focus. Even handicapped without a full review of the Memory File, I was still in control, after all. This Vacation should be no different. My attraction to Evangeline had just thrown me off my game a bit, that's all.

* * *

I suppose, before I go any further, I should speak a bit about my world. I need to explain the beliefs that shaped my initial actions during this last Vacation, as it was the loss of those same beliefs that set me on the path to my ultimate fall from grace. Or rise to grace, depending on your perspective, I guess.

I know all Earthbounds have imagined what heaven might be like, should it exist. While none of my kind call it that, our god "home" is still a pleasant enough place, I suppose.

Don't get too excited. For all those angels, rapturous music, and reunions with lost loved ones or any other bliss Earthbounds have imagined for themselves? There's none of that where I come from.

What there is for us gods is just this: no responsibilities, no stress, no worries. Just being.

While this may sound blissful to some of you, I think any honest god would tell you it is a bit dull. Too comfortable, too laid back, too bland, too everything. That's why we go Earthbound. So your chaotic lives can provide us with some much needed distraction from our peaceful, uneventful eternity.

What do we do with all that freedom back home? Mostly, we just sit around, talking. When not on Vacation, we jokingly call home "no-man's-land," as we seem to be stuck in a state of permanent stasis.

Think of it as a celestial Starbucks. A massive, never-ending, typically crowded coffee-house filled with a sea of dull faces and bored expressions, all sipping overly complex drinks with nothing else significant going on. Over, and over, and over for all time. Starting to get my drift? Relaxing and appealing in small doses, sure, but not for eternity. We try to pass the time chatting, but most of our conversations, in my opinion, are uninspired.

Thankfully, we have gods Playground to take us away from it all. From the stress of no stress. Plus, our Vacations also give us something to talk about when we get back.

Just in case it still sounds appealing to you, I might as well tell you; I don't think Earthbounds make it. Gods are just gods. We've always been, and always will be. If there is a special place, a "heaven" just for you, I've never seen it.

* * *

As I expected, the inside of the pub was just as dark and gloomy as the outside. She led us to the corner booth, waving at the barkeep.

He gave a deferential nod, yelling, "Hey gorgeous," before turning to pour some drinks.

Clearing my throat, I tried to ignore the heavy smoke and smell of beer that permeated the room.

The bartender arrived, slamming two tall drafts on the table.

"The usual, Hun?"

She nodded as she shrugged off her burgundy coat, revealing a simple, form-fitting black dress. He reached out to touch her shoulder.

"Sorry about Constantine," he slurred. "Inevitable, I guess. You hang in there, kiddo."

She looked up at the scruffy, obese man and then surprised us both as a single tear escaped down her cheek.

Swatting it away angrily, she snapped, "Best rid of him, anyway. Doomed from the start, we were." She lifted her gaze to smile apologetically at me.

"This is Adam. He's an old childhood friend of Constantine's."

"Didn't think Constantine had any friends. Pleasure to meet ya," the barkeep said dismissively, already turning away to return to his station.

"So...."

She gave her twisted smile to me again, then waited. She looked like an angel. A sad, fallen, lost, confused angel in a very tight dress.

I tried to relax. I allowed myself to slump a bit in the booth, unsure if Adam would be uncomfortable or able to settle into such an environment.

"So, your name is Ava?"

"Evangeline. Like I told you at the cemetery." She gave me a look that said she wasn't used to people forgetting her name. "My mother had a thing for old Greek stuff. It means 'bearer of good news,' or something like that. Not really fitting, right? I'm certainly nobody's good news." The fire fell away from her tone.

"What? No, I'm sure it's a lovely name."

She was staring dispassionately at me. I felt the need to keep speaking, to keep her attention.

"You want to know more about Constantine and me as children?" I quickly scanned the Memory Upload, looking for an amusing or charming story to tell.

"There was this one time when we were about ten. We skipped school so we could go watch the baseball game...."

Placing her hand on my forearm, she smiled weakly.

"Sorry, changed my mind. I don't think there's anything you could tell me about Constantine, the child, that would change my opinion of Constantine, the man."

She sighed. "Why don't you tell me about yourself? Who is Adam? What do you do, and why did you come here?"

She'd done it again. Thrown me for a loop. This Possession was the most unnerving I'd experienced in ages. I felt out of control, unprepared. A lesson in too quick a turn-around, I suppose. I really should have read that Memory File.

"I...."

I should push the panic button and get pulled the hell out of here! Instead, I leaned closer so I could smell her scent again.

"I run an advertising firm. In Chicago."

I tried to look contemplative. "Constantine and I were always bouncing crazy ideas off one another as kids, our inspirations for inventions and businesses we wanted to start. We both wanted to run our own companies one day."

Evangeline offered me a doubtful smile, her lips pursing.

"Then you both reached your goal. If nothing else, Constantine was a man in charge of his own destiny. Different businesses, but both still the boss."

I shifted on the hard bench uncomfortably. Adam and Constantine had obviously taken very different life paths, and I was certain Adam would disapprove of Constantine's choices.

Evangeline reached out to grasp both my hands across the table.

"Sorry, I'm being very unfair to you. You've done nothing to deserve my bitterness." She sighed.

"I'm sure you're a lovely, successful person. You're a good friend to come, especially after all this time." She paused. "Nice suit."

She began to finger the edge of my jacket sleeve, trailing her finger along the tiny threads of the hem's stitching. We were mercifully interrupted by the barkeep's return. He placed two steaming plates on the table.

Evangeline began to eat hungrily, taking large mouthfuls of the mixture of limp vegetables mixed with a mound of unrecognizable meat.

"Aren't you hungry? Eat up; it's good. Liver with a honey ambrosia sauce. The food of the gods, they say."

"Ha!" I choked. "Never heard that. Food of the gods, eh?" I began to push the unappealing mess around with my fork.

Now, if I'm being totally truthful, one of the main reasons that we gods come down to earth for Vacation is not just for adventure and excitement; we come for the food.

Where we exist, we don't have a need for such things, but we all admit we miss it. Food is fun, pleasurable. Tasting is an exquisite decadence. In our world, while we don't eat, we do have access to a tasteless drink – other gods think it is provided as a distraction, or perhaps works as some sort of 'god fuel.' My personal theory is that it ensures we take turns while conversing; the opportunity to jump in while another sips.

That being said, I have been down to earth over a hundred times, and I know I hate liver. Fried liver, minced liver, liver and onions…. it didn't matter. I find it distasteful in all its forms.

After several minutes of silence, she was finished. I couldn't get over her appetite for such a small person.

"You're not going to eat? Do you want anything else?" She reached across the table, stuffing her fork into my plate.

"No, nothing for me. I'm not that hungry. It was a long trip here. I guess I'm just tired."

"Sure, you are. Where are you staying? Maybe we could go there for a cocktail — you can tell me more about yourself before we call it a night."

As captivating as Evangeline was, I couldn't decipher why she was latching on to me. What was her story? Why this strange interest in Adam given how she apparently felt about her boyfriend, Constantine?

Plus, I had no idea where I was staying. Damn my incomplete Memory Upload! I sent up an urgent request, begging for more data.

She was doing it again. Staring at me with that bemused, perceptive look that seemed to imply she knew exactly what I was thinking. Like she knew I was pretending.

"You *are* staying somewhere in town." More staring.

Ha! It came to me. Saved yet again by the Playground Controller.

"Yes. At The Plaza, the Fairmont hotel at 59th & 5th." I was pleased to provide the answer.

She rolled her eyes, then stood up.

"Well, Mr. 'at the Plaza,' shall we be off then?"

I looked around, searching for pub staff. Seeing only the same bartender, I walked up to the bar. Reaching into my jacket pocket, I pulled out the wallet that I'd felt pressing against my chest.

Before I could pull out any cash, he waved me off.

"On the house, on account of Constantine's death and all," he grumbled. He peered at me with disapproval through the bar's haze.

"Thank you."

Evangeline was bending over the booth, reaching for her coat. I turned back to the barkeep, intending to shake his hand before returning to her side.

Then I felt it. A premonition. That tingling, animal-instinct on the back of your neck.

We gods don't have such survival programming. We're above the need to ward off predators. When in Possession of

26

a human Host, however, we experience the world as they would have experienced it. That warning bell I was sensing was the gift of primal fear. I've learned over the years that this subcortical instinct is very real and surprisingly reliable. It shouldn't be ignored.

It is almost always right.

Instead of completing my turn, I leapt over the bar, crashing into the bartender, and took us both down behind the bar front in a tangle of limbs and cries.

Ping! Ttt-ttt-ttt-ttt-ttt.

The echo of gunshots shattered the bar's gloom and the barkeep gasped. His lazy eyes now wide with terror, he stared at me, his mouth agape.

Liquor bottles shattered above me on the wall, raining glass and liquid down upon us. Shaking off the panicking barman, I began to crawl along the floor to the edge of the bar. I winced as I felt several glass shards pierce my arms and legs. The unpleasantness of the body!

A trickle of liquid rolled down my face, partially blinding me. I raised one arm to wipe it away; my hand came back red.

As I leaned forward to carefully peer around the end of the bar through the dim haze, at first, all I could hear was uncontrolled screams — that sound of complete chaos that arises when humans are in desperate fear for their lives.

Then I spotted her.

Evangeline was crouched under the booth table, curled up as small as she could make herself against the wall beneath the booth. Her lips were parted as she panted in fear, and her eyes flared with the intensity of an animal caught in a corner, panicked and afraid.

Three men dressed in dark suits were advancing into the room. They all had guns. By my estimate, either Glocks or Barettas — which they were shooting throughout the room.

If they did have an intended target, they were not entirely sure who or where that person was, or at least that's how it appeared to me. They seemed to be covering their bases by attempting to shoot as many people as possible.

How to save her?

I had no choice. I broke protocol with gods Playground rules yet again, and Body Jumped.

The assassin I entered was surprisingly strong of mind. He vehemently resisted the Possession, but after some concentrated effort, I was able to wrest control of his body and mind from him.

Adam, meanwhile, collapsed behind the bar, confused, gasping. I needed to return to him before he did anything stupid.

New me, this trivial hitman, this assassin, stopped shooting at the bar's patrons. I spun around and began to shoot at my own comrades, at the two men who had entered the bar with me.

It was over in seconds. Caught completely unprepared for their associate's new intentions, I was able to shoot them both unchallenged. Using my new Host's marksmanship skills, I shot the first in the back, the second in the head. They both fell dead where they stood, crumbling to the floor like puppets without their master.

I planted the urge in my temporary Host to run out the door, then captured Adam's gaze. I abandoned my gun-wielding Host to leap quickly back into Adam.

As the bewildered gunman fled, Adam crawled out from behind the bar, calling out to Evangeline.

"Evangeline! Are you ok?"

Sobbing, she emerged from beneath the booth, all personal bravado forgotten.

"Adam, I'm so sorry. They must be seeking revenge. Constantine's death mustn't have been enough to satisfy them."

She grasped my bloody hand. "We need to get out of here before they come back!"

Nodding, I pulled her along with me as I stood up, looking around the bar. Miraculously, other than the two hoodlums I'd shot, no other motionless bodies were apparent. I saw one patron who'd been hit, holding his bleeding leg, and another checking his grazed arm. A third woman was grasping her shoulder, but I didn't see a lot of blood. Everyone else was slowly finding their feet, dazed but not seriously hurt.

Clinging to my arm, Evangeline whispered, "No one in town knows who you are. Take me to your hotel. We can hide there until I figure out what to do next. You'll help me?"

She turned two enormous, imploring eyes up towards me, her desperate expression still warm and brave.

"We're getting out of here," I agreed. "Come on."

Together we walked out the door, hand in hand, leaving the chaos behind us. As we emerged into the refreshing cool air of the evening, I realized I had never felt so alive.

When you are a creature blessed with eternal life, feeling this alive was unexpected. A true curiosity. This was a big deal. Like the ultimate luxury vacation or the perfect gift.

This was my best Possession ever, and it was all because of Evangeline.

*   *   *

Investigative Report by god Policeman #632
re Protocol Breach: Body Jumping
– Offending god: #201

The Controller reported a possible breach of gods Playground Rules by #201 early on during his Adam Juri Vacation.

Breach: Suspected Body Jump.

The required subsequent investigation, however, was unfortunately delayed. A full review of the three human hitmen's Memory Files was completed a few days later, and these provided indisputable evidence that #201 had indeed discovered Body Jumping.

Unfortunately, this information did not come to light until after #201 had reached the end of his Vacation allotment. As such, our Recall agents were not aware of his abilities when they encountered #201 during their first collection attempt on the plane, and they were caught unprepared.

Steps have been taken to rectify this problem, such that similar instances of miscommunication and delay in information transfer between the Controller's personnel and the god Police Agents will not arise in the future.

(Resumption of #201 narrative)

* * *

A short while later, I pulled up to the towering Plaza hotel, its golden-lit front sparkling welcomingly under the added shadows of the streetlights.

I hopped out and ran around to get the door for Evangeline. She'd seemed to compose herself on the drive, although she'd said almost nothing.

As I looked around to inquire about parking, the bellhop said from over my shoulder, "Welcome back, Mr. Juri."

I nodded, pretending I knew where I was and handed him the keys. I then gestured for Evangeline to follow me into the hotel.

As we pushed through the front revolving door, I reached out to touch her arm gently.

"How are you feeling? Do you want to go to the room and lie down?"

Smiling weakly, she shrugged as though I'd asked if she was tired on New Year's Eve.

"No, I'm fine now. Why don't we go sit somewhere and chat?"

Nodding, I led her to the hotel's Rose Club, the lounge overlooking the lobby.

As we sank into two cushy chairs in the corner, I wondered how to broach the subject of the bar shooting. While Evangeline had already admitted she thought she'd been the intended target, she hadn't elaborated further during our drive.

Instead of confronting her immediately, I picked up a few table napkins and began dabbing at my various cuts.

"I think they have a live jazz band playing here tonight. This hotel has quite the history, actually. Many of the greats played here, like Miles Davis, Duke Ellington...." my mind drifted as I stared into her eyes, lost in my reaction to this creature. I was unsure how to proceed.

There was that crooked grin again. "Before my time, I think. But jazz sounds nice, distracting."

The waiter brought us some nuts, barely glancing at my cuts. I ordered us two Cosmopolitans and was soon sipping nervously on my drink once it arrived.

With each passing minute, I was torn. The plan had been just a quick peek, to attend the funeral, then make a quick exit and finish off the Vacation back in Adam's world, far from anyone I may have interacted with while living as Constantine.

However, nothing about my reaction to this woman Evangeline was typical, and with each passing moment, my thoughts were becoming more and more unsettled. On the one hand, I felt a pressing urge to leave, to abort the entire Vacation. On the other, I couldn't take my eyes off her, and I felt an overwhelming desire to have Adam stay in her world, to save her from whatever fate had in store.

Strange. I wasn't used to this urge to protect an Earthbound. Other than preserving our own Host, we gods pretty much focus on our own amusement during our brief stay — no time to take on dependents or concern ourselves with the lives of surrounding Earthbounds.

Regardless, there was another reason I had to stick around. I had a bet to win.

A few Vacation rounds ago, back home during one of those many drawn-out, tedious time-killing conversations, I'd made a bet regarding this very thing. To be clear, not a wager about any concern for or assistance of Earthbounds, but rather about the concept of engagement with other Earthbounds in a way meaningful to we gods.

I'd initially made the bet out of boredom I think, or perhaps more honestly, out of irritation, but either way, I was committed to winning the bet. My unexpected infatuation with Evangeline shouldn't derail me from my mission. Perhaps, she could even play a vital part in my plans to win my wager.

On the day I took on the challenge, a group of we gods were just sitting about, sipping our drinks and talking as usual, when the conversation turned to the topic of surrounding players during a Vacation.

While residing in a Host, it can be a challenge to predict and manage the reactions and behaviors of the surrounding Earthbound Participants. Every god knows this but works around it during their stay. They tend to do this by studying the Memory File of their current Host or by only engaging with other Earthbounds they encounter in superficial ways.

"Earthbounds, when not Hosting, are unmanageable, and their behavior is impossible to predict," said one god.

"Likely, this is why our Vacations are kept so short. It is unavoidable," offered another, "given the changeable and irrational nature of Earthbounds."

Several other gods nodded. "Illogical beings," one said. "Emotional time bombs," agreed another.

Until then, I'd been sitting slumped in my too comfortable chair, passively listening, stirring my drink, waiting for something exciting to happen or for my next Vacation Request to be called up. Now I had a reason to speak.

"I disagree."

They all fell silent and stared at me.

"It is possible to manage other Earthbounds, to manipulate surrounding Participants' behavior. I've done it," I bragged.

A lie, but as I said, I was bored.

The god sitting across from me shook his head.

"Control an Earthbound beyond your current Host? There's no way. Without Suppression, all Earthbounds are loose cannons. They break their own rules, go against logic, or violate their own best interests all too often. Albeit some more frequently than others, sure, but as a breed, they're too volatile for any god to fully control from the outside."

My irritation with their arrogance was what had initially caused me to speak up, but now I was warming to my own idea.

"I didn't say control, I said manage. I can manage to influence the behavior and actions of surrounding Earthbounds while residing in a nearby Host. They're open to influence, particularly if you read their desires and fears correctly."

I smiled. I hadn't really done this before, not to any true extent, but who doesn't like a challenge to spice up eternity? Why not up the ante, as they say?

I sat up and spread my hands wide. "Who wants to bet that I can be the ultimate puppet master?"

Several of the surrounding gods exchanged smirks.

"Sure, 201, I'll take that bet." "Me too," said another.

The game was on. "Great. Let's say I get the next five Visitations to prove my concept. I'll come back with proof that I can manipulate and control multiple Earthbounds to my own ends and desires. Without any god tricks, without risking revealing my presence in my Host."

Several gods agreed to take on the bet. Should I succeed, all participating gods would have to forfeit their next Vacation for my use. Winning would more than double my Vacation allotment for the next few years. If I lost, I'd give up my rights to my own pending Vacations for the next year, to be shared across my opponents.

So... given my actual goal, it bore to reason that I could try to help Evangeline; if only so I could show that I could control her and any other players in her story. I would manipulate her against her best interests at some point — to prove that I was in control of not just Adam, but also Evangeline.

I couldn't afford to lose; I'd been down three times already since the bet, but despite my best efforts, had failed to gather sufficient evidence to clinch the win. With just this Vacation and one other left in my challenge, it was crunch time. There was no way I was going to chance getting stuck in our heavenly Starbucks for the next twelve months.

I wouldn't get very far with my plans, however, if Evangeline didn't start telling me the truth. I needed to gain her trust if I was going to be able to direct her future.

She saved me from my own conflicted thoughts by breaking the silence.

"So, Adam Juri. Now that I've fed you a horrible lunch and gotten you shot at, you know almost everything there is to know about me." Evangeline smiled wearily.

"I'm the uneducated girlfriend of your old friend who turned gangster. A lonely girl with bad taste in food, and apparently someone who now has a price on her head."

She leaned closer to me until our knees almost touched.

"So, let's cut to the chase. Who are you? Why are you still here? Why didn't you remain at the bar and talk to the police? Why help me run away?"

She stared at me curiously. "Shouldn't you be fleeing from this horrible mess, back to your normal, safe life?"

Ha! She was trying to turn the tables on me, offering a deft preemptive strike against my own pending questions.

Leaning closer across the small bar table, I whispered, "It'll be ok, Evangeline. I'll help you. You'll see."

Her eyes widened in surprise. She sat back, sinking into the deep leather cushions as though trying to disappear within their folds. Once again, a tear betrayed the resigned veneer she offered, and she wiped it away angrily with the sleeve of her dress.

"I'm fine. I don't need your help. I've been taking care of myself for years, for as long as I can remember, actually."

I took another sip of my drink. "What about your family, your parents?" I asked gently. "Do you have somewhere you could go?"

Laughing sharply, she took a long sip of her own drink, staring cautiously around the bar.

"I don't know my family. Whoever they were, they didn't want me. I grew up in foster homes and learned a long time ago that you can trust no one in this world – no one except yourself."

She spun her head back around to stare intently into my eyes. "That's enough about me."

Once again, she leaned closer. This time her eyes narrowed like a cat's, and she tilted her head slightly as she studied my face.

"You're a strange one, Adam Juri. You dress all fancy, you look like an elitist, and yet here you are, hanging out with your dead friend's criminal girlfriend. Why didn't you jump to call the cops after we were shot at in the bar?"

Damn! She wasn't giving up, and she was actually right. I was likely acting out of character for Adam.

"Well, I...." Drawing on my best creative abilities, I came up with a response that I felt was inspired.

"Constantine was the only real close friend I ever had in life. We were always there for each other. I feel like I owe him somehow."

Evangeline's nose crinkled, and I realized she needed more convincing.

"I know that may seem strange to you and that you think we're very different people, but Constantine was a terrific friend to me growing up — like a brother. We had a lot more in common than you may think. I feel like he'd want me to look out for you, to help you."

Evangeline studied me for a moment longer. I put on my best poker face, meeting her stare head-on.

She shrugged. "Ok, fine. So you're one of the good guys and want to pay back your friend. Whatever. So, what do you really want from me in return?"

Now I was confused again. Want? I wanted nothing, everything, just to be near her, anything she would throw my way.

Wait, that was my attraction talking. What I truly wanted, what I needed, was to show I could control her; I needed to win my bet. Yet... I felt the pull of that strange protective urge again.

I think you humans call it love at first sight. I have no idea how it feels to you, but the attraction I felt was all-consuming. Intoxicating, heady, maybe dangerous.

I had no business falling for an Earthbound. I was on a mission. If I couldn't succeed, if I was too distracted, then I really should go home. This was a bonus trip, after all, under the radar. I couldn't waste the opportunity to prove that I was the true Puppet Master.

"Just let me help you. Help you sort this out, whatever it is. For Constantine. Ok?"

She gave me another weak smile. She suddenly looked exhausted.

"Sure, Adam. Help me. First up, I think we both need some sleep."

She got up and began walking across the room. Several men and women at other tables watched her walk by. Even tired and in shock, she was a vision difficult to ignore.

"You coming?"

She cast a soft, teasing look over her shoulder, then, without waiting for my response, continued to walk out of the bar and towards the elevators.

I leapt to my feet, quickly dropping several large bills on the table. I also pulled out the room keycard that I'd seen protruding from my wallet earlier. I realized that I didn't know what room I was staying in.

I wasn't sure what to do next or who was manipulating who, but I knew I wasn't going anywhere without Evangeline.

Two
WHO'S USING WHO?

I was saved the embarrassment of asking the desk clerk for my room number by the arrival of the manager, who came rushing up to greet me as I exited the lounge.

"Mr. Juri, you've returned. Once again, I'm so sorry the room was not to your satisfaction earlier. I've moved your luggage to the new suite, which I personally oversaw."

He clasped his two hands together. "I think you'll find everything in order. I'm certain the new Fitzgerald Suite will meet with your satisfaction. I took the liberty of placing some Jazz CDs in the sound system, as well as stocking the fridge with your usual preferences…."

His voice trailed off as he tuned in to my appearance.

He stared with unmasked curiosity at the series of small cuts across my forehead and lacing the back of my hands, then looked up and down my crumpled suit. I straightened my spine and stared back.

Recovering his professional composure, he reached towards me to extend a small envelope that he had clutched in one hand.

"Here's the new room key card. You can take the gold elevators directly to the 18th floor."

The manager now paused, glancing at Evangeline, who had walked back to join us. Clearing his throat, he added, "Does your… friend have any luggage that I can assist with?"

Adam would no doubt find this all terribly embarrassing, I thought.

"Her luggage was lost," I replied sternly. "Please send up some suitable toiletries for her and a blouse and slacks from your Douglas Hannant boutique downstairs. Size 2."

Evangeline gave me a surprised look. I'd guessed her size correctly, then.

I cleared my throat, adding for effect, "If the luggage doesn't arrive by morning, we will have an excuse to explore your wonderful shops ourselves."

"Of course, sir," he replied. Any conclusions he'd drawn were now in doubt as his expression was artfully respectful.

Taking Evangeline's arm, I guided her away from the curious manager and towards the far elevator.

As we stepped inside and the mirrored doors slid softly together, she leaned into me, whispering, "Thanks for that. Judgmental prick, wasn't he?"

I coughed, still unaccustomed to her bluntness. It was in such contrast to her angelic beauty and disarming sweet nature. What's the expression, "you can never judge a book by its cover?" Evangeline was a myriad of contradictions for me, a walking puzzle.

At once harsh as she was soft, at once strong as she was so obviously broken. While none of this could fully explain my deep attraction to her, I felt that I needed to learn more. It felt important that I help her.

Then the call came.

God #201! A reminder that this Vacation is set to expire in 36 hours. Please confirm receipt.

I wanted to ignore the Controller, but of course, that was impossible. *Understood,* I replied telepathically and then broke the connection to return my attention to Evangeline. I gave her an awkward hug.

"My pleasure, Evangeline," I said softly, staring over her head at Adam's reflection in the elevator mirror. I looked tired but also determined.

I had a feeling I might need to miss the Playground Recall time. At least by a little bit.

* * *

When we arrived at the room, I swung the double doors wide. Evangeline pushed past me into the room, then gasped.

"Wow! You travel in style, Adam Juri! Look at that domed ceiling and those glass chandeliers. Constantine liked to live large, but he never took me to any place like this! Are all these things real antiques or replicas? Very 'Art Deco,' right?"

Without waiting for a reply, she began to run about the suite, exploring every nook and cranny like she'd just won the lottery. Little squeals of surprise and joy escaped between a rush of unnecessary commentary, for I could see everything as well as her and did not require the detailed description that was pouring from her lips.

"Adam! Have you seen your bathroom? I think these fixtures are real gold plated! And all this marble, it's gorgeous. Oh, my god! There's *another* flat-screen TV in here! *Who* watches TV in the bathroom?"

As I entered the bedroom, Evangeline came bursting back out of the vanity suite with a lush, white terry robe, which she had already wrapped over her dress. "It's official. You can have the bed. I'll sleep in the bathroom."

I smiled, enjoying her exuberance. I'd stayed in many luxury suites over the years, in many much grander than this one, in fact. While not all visits to gods Playground were high-end, I was definitely much more jaded to such trinkets and flashy amenities than my new roommate.

Mistaking my expression for disapproval, Evangeline said, "Relax, stuffy head. I'm just kidding. You've got to appreciate the day, though, right?"

Appreciate the day? What was she talking about? She couldn't possibly have already forgotten our near brush with death!

Rather than explain herself to me, Evangeline walked over to the minibar.

"Let's see what your big shot profile led our nosy Manager to stock for you." Once again, she employed her sultry tone.

When her face came back up from behind the fridge door, a teasing grin danced across her face, and her eyes sparkled in the most disarming way possible.

"Well, well, well, I never would have pegged you for *one of those.*" Evangeline laughed as she stood up, one hand behind her back.

I was confused. What could Adam have possibly requested be placed in the fridge that she would find so amusing? Worse, I should know this, but once again, I hadn't read the Memory Upload and was missing the information I now needed.

"Well, I...." as I struggled to form a suitable response, I turned nervously to look out the bedroom window.

"You can see most of 58th street from here," I said lamely, hoping she would drop the game.

Walking closer to join me by the window, Evangeline kept her hand hidden behind her robe.

"You *do* know what was in the fridge, right?" she asked, her voice now only half teasing.

"Evangeline, I...."

Pulling her hand abruptly out from behind her back, she proudly held up a tall clear bottle filled with a white liquid.

"They left you a note too. 'Dear Mr. Juri, please find a warming plate on the side shelf for your evening milk. Sincerely, the Management.' " Evangeline laughed.

"Need your warm glass of milk before bed, do you? Should I warm it for you, or do you prefer to complete that ritual yourself, pussy cat?"

Have mercy! Adam was full of unwanted surprises. I really should have reviewed his Memory Files before coming down. I quickly scanned his files but didn't find anything useful.

So, I lied.

"If you must know, it's an old habit from before my mother died. We were really close, and she was a remarkable person, full of stories and wisdom. When I was a child, we would sit by the fire together and have a glass of warm milk and a chat for a few minutes before we went to bed each night. It was my favorite time of the day."

Evangeline's expression softened, and her tone became regretful. "I'm so sorry. Sometimes I get carried away with my teasing and forget to think. When did your mother pass away?"

Luckily, this memory *was* available to me.

"Shortly after I left for University. It was a long time ago. And there is no need for you to apologize. There was no way for you to know."

I walked over to the closet and grabbed a blanket from the top shelf.

"We should get some sleep. You can have the bed, Evangeline. I'll take the couch."

Without looking back, I left the bedroom and went back into the sitting room, flicking off the light on my way out.

* * *

This may come as a surprise, but we gods still sleep.

When we're in the middle of a Possession, we do, I mean. Bound by the limits of the Host body, we eventually need to allow the Host to rest, to recharge enough to function optimally for our purposes.

While still partially alert, our own awareness is pushed into a less active state during Host sleep. This is because all the inbound input is filtered and weak; we're taking in less information through all of the senses. Think of it like being trapped in a small room with a blindfold and earmuffs on while you wait for someone else to come release you from the dark.

When the suite doors at the end of the sitting room burst open a few hours later, I didn't know what was happening at first. Luckily Adam awoke, and I quickly took over his consciousness and senses as I tried to get my bearings.

The lights from the city below cast an eerie glow through the thin window sheers, and I stumbled over the coffee table in my effort to get off the couch quickly.

My clumsiness proved to be a lifesaver for Evangeline.

A figure had been cautiously advancing through the sitting room towards her bedroom, apparently also somewhat blinded by the dim light. He had not noticed me on the couch, but upon hearing my fall across the coffee table, he aborted his advance and whirled about in surprise towards me.

No longer intent on entering the bedroom, he stepped back towards the couch and the window. I crouched low to the floor, hoping I was at least partially obscured by the table and the night shadows.

As my eyes slowly adjusted to the dim light, I realized that the large man had raised his two arms high above his head. In his hands was clasped something long and thin. A stick? Broom? Shotgun?

Then he brought his arms down upon the center of the antique coffee table, and the sound of splintering wood filled the night.

Tire iron, I thought, as I rolled away from the table to take up a new spot behind the couch.

Without speaking or uttering a threat, the monstrous man swung again.

This time his blow caused the couch to topple backward, and I couldn't help but yelp in surprise.

I dashed across the room towards the kitchenette, desperate to find some sort of weapon of my own.

In this way, we danced about the room for several moments, although it felt much longer. My pursuer continued to swing and strike with somewhat random fury. Luckily for me, his aim was horrible.

Glass shattered as his tire iron met with the antique mirrors, artwork, framed photographs, and decorative trophy urns that adorned the suite's walls and shelves. The collection of books that had been on the side shelves now flew about the room like a mob of angry, flapping birds, and the entire scene began to take on a surreal tone for me. I was surprised by my own fear and shock. I was used to more controlled reactions during Vacations.

Can she seriously be sleeping through all of this? There had been no movement nor sound from the nearby bedroom, at least none that I could discern.

Normally more intuitive and calculating, I, unfortunately, misjudged the thug's next movements and ended up cornered by the sitting room's ensuite bathroom.

I wasn't as excited by the thought of dying as I'd been just two days ago. I had other plans at the moment, and dying just didn't fit in.

"Are you sure you've got the right guy?" I blurted as I twisted in the corner, hoping to slide along the wall past him. A lame effort at best.

Lame or not, my sudden words appeared to catch my pursuer by surprise, for he hesitated mid-swing.

That was enough.

A looming shape appeared behind him, and then something came crashing down on the man's skull.

He fell as silently to the floor as he'd been throughout our scuffle, barely making more than a thump as his body folded onto the suite's plush carpet.

"Adam? Are you alright?"

Her whispered voice cracked slightly, all sultriness forgotten.

"Evangeline?"

I reached out to flip on the hall light and stared incredulously at my petite companion, who stood perched atop a large armchair, looking down at the floor where the large, slumped man lay before it. She was panting with exertion as she stared down at her victim.

In her hand was clutched a rather large, cast-iron bookend.

"Is that the Brooklyn Bridge?" I croaked, still catching my own breath.

Evangeline looked down at the item in her hands as if it were a foreign object, as though she had no clue how it had come to be there.

Looking back up at me, she smiled. "So it is. Talk about tacky."

She let the bookend fall to the floor before melting to the ground herself, sliding off the chair.

I rushed over to her side and gently helped her to sit back in the armchair, which was one of the few chairs still standing.

"You saved my life." I turned, confirming our assailant was still unconscious.

She brushed her long hair back from her face. "Then I guess that makes us even, sort of." She began to shake.

Noticing for the first time that she was dressed only in her undergarments, I dashed to the nearby washroom and quickly returned with one of the plush bathrobes, plus the belt off of a second robe. After tying the thug's hands with the extra strap, I turned and wrapped Evangeline in the robe. As I began to search the kitchenette for something else to tie his feet with as well, I wondered what she believed had happened yesterday in the pub.

"Well, I can't really take any credit for our escape from the pub shootout yesterday," I said carefully.

I couldn't find anything but a couple of tea towels, so I did my best to secure his feet with them as I talked.

"Those guys seemed to be confused, hitting each other like that, and the last one fled without any encouragement from me. We just got lucky."

When she didn't respond, I added, "But you and my old friend Constantine sure seem to know how to make dangerous enemies. I just wish I knew how they figured out where to find us." I thought for a moment.

"They must have seen us leave the funeral together and managed to identify me somehow. Or perhaps they followed us."

The sun was just beginning to rise outside the far window, and the dawning light highlighted the angles of Evangeline's face, accentuating the roundness of her cheekbones and lips. As she smiled her troubled smile at me, I thought again how different this Possession was from any other Vacation I had ever taken.

"A faraway world from your normal stomping ground, I bet." She gestured towards the slumped thug without looking at him too closely.

"Is he dead? Did I kill him?"

I leaned in closer to him and felt the caress of his exhale on my neck, which was somehow surprisingly gentle for such a large man. I shook my head.

"No, he's still alive. You definitely knocked him out cold, though."

"Thank goodness. I've never killed anyone before, and I don't want to start."

I could see her hands shaking as she ran them through her hair again.

"If you want to leave, I'll understand."

Rising to her feet, she pulled the robe tighter around her and began to walk back towards the bedroom.

Although she was no longer looking at me, I shook my head.

"Well then, if you're still planning to be my hero, you'd better figure out what to do with our slumbering friend and this mess. Then we need to get out of here, pronto."

I smiled. She'd never turned around. She'd sensed I'd stay.

Then she did turn back. She stared intently at me, her green eyes flashing as they reflected the fading moonlight through the far window.

"Constantine's enemies are definitely out for revenge, and clearly, his death wasn't enough —now they want mine as well. I need to get out of New York. I need to disappear."

I checked again to ensure our attacker was still unconscious.

"Agreed. Go ahead and freshen up. I'll put our friend to sleep on the couch and clean up in here as best I can."

I looked wryly around at the devastation of the regal suite.

"I don't think the Plaza's going to allow Adam Juri back here any time soon."

Evangeline threw me her twisted grin again.

"Do you always talk about yourself in the third person, Adam?"

Caught in my mistake, I silently chided myself for the error.

"Just the shock of it all, I guess," I offered with a weak chuckle.
"Alright, *Adam Juri,* if you're really going to stick by your promise to help your old friend's girl, then we'd better get going before daylight."

I nodded. I needed to know more about her, who she was inside. She was unlike any other Earthbound woman I'd ever met.

Finally, after all my Vacations, something unique. *I'm infatuated with an Earthbound. Never thought it would happen to me.*

Every god knows one fact. Eternity can be dull at times. Unfulfilling, even.

But now I had Evangeline.

I was overjoyed.

* * *

I should probably explain about the Body Jumping and the killing of Earthbounds.

Body Jumping is the easier one to explain. I'm sure you're wondering why I didn't use this cute trick to defeat the midnight thug after I'd so easily employed it during the pub shootout.

For starters, I only stumbled upon the possibility of Body Jumping last year while on another Vacation — while living the life of a powerful business tycoon.

At least, that's how he was described in the Playground Menu. When I chose him, I'd assumed that his life would be a thrilling escape, when in actuality, it turned out to be a rather dull trip — the realities of the business world, even at the highest levels, were nowhere near as glamorous on a day-to-day basis as I would have expected based on your romanticizing of such people in the media and television. I sometimes forget that we gods are not the only creatures fond of fantasies and escapism as it relates to their own existence.

In any event, that particular mundane trip took a more entertaining turn on the second afternoon, over a long business lunch.

My Host was meeting with a second associate who'd brought along his girlfriend. A remarkably dull girl, but "easy to look at," I suppose.

As lunch dragged on and the drinks flowed, I experienced a spark of joy when I realized the girlfriend was keeping a secret. What, I didn't know, but her every glance, the nervous tick above her lip, her shrill laugh; everything about her told me she was hiding something.

Dirty secrets can make for great puzzles, and I was intrigued to know what she was hiding. So intrigued that I began to focus intently on her as I wondered what anxious, confused story was racing behind her jittery, shallow eyes.

Imagine my surprise when I suddenly saw my own Host's body sitting across from me, gasping and sweating, staring about in confusion! It took me a second to realize that I'd accidentally abandoned him and somehow ended up in the twitching tart.

I quickly refocused on my bewildered businessman and managed to return to him within moments. In my own alarm, I didn't even pause long enough to learn the girl's secret, which I now regret.

Since then, I've only dared Body Jump one other time, which was yesterday, in the pub.

When I returned home from the businessman's Possession, I did try to feel out the Controller, to find out if the experience was unique — I wanted to know if other gods could do it.

Unfortunately, the Controller wasn't as chatty that day and didn't take the bait. It took me ages to suss out the rumor mill, but I eventually learned that I wasn't the only one who'd stumbled upon this "Body Jumping" option.

Actually, it was fairly simple to enact; Jumping only required a brief moment of intense focus on the new Host. Just a second of undeterred and undivided attention within a moment of eye contact. Kind of hard to do in the dark, though.

Unfortunately, I also found out that any form of Body Jumping was strictly forbidden. Further, the discovery that you had employed Jumping could result in your "Vacation termination." Rumor had it would not be just for that trip, but indefinitely.

Then, there are the side effects.

Most troublesome is the return to consciousness of your original Host before your intended departure. This, of course, can prove horribly problematic should you intend to return to your Host, as typically, when our presence departs, they are prone to doing and saying bizarre things.

This odd behavior is not surprising, of course, since at the end of a normal Vacation, the Host is returning to consciousness three days later, and usually in a different location from when we first took Possession.

To reduce the aftereffects of our Possessions, the Controller typically implants our travel memories into the Host, thereby filling in the "missing period" of time. While these foreign memories usually feel off or incomplete, they are typically enough to stop most Hosts from discussing their confusion with others. Even when they realize they've acted out of character, nobody wants to sound crazy after already appearing atypical.

This reprogramming, however, can take several minutes. Before the Controller's done, the Host's "resurfacing anxiety" can result in all sorts of aberrant behavior.

So, it is my conclusion that leaving a primary Host (even temporarily) while Body Jumping inflicts a highly undesirable period of panic and confusion. There's no telling what they'll do or say before you return. This means that reclaiming the same Host and continuing the Vacation without arousing suspicions of mental illness would be almost impossible.

Luckily, back at the pub, Evangeline was too busy being shot at to notice Adam's sputtering or his unique confusion before I was able to return to him. Plus, in all the chaos, he'd certainly had no chance to interact with anyone else before we reunited.

I only hoped the Controller hadn't caught it. I don't even know if she could, but the rumors certainly implied it was best not to find out.

Whether the Controller was wise to me or not, I had a sneaking feeling that my new adventure, this glorious mystery that was Evangeline, may require me to break a few more rules. It might get me into a bit of trouble before I was done.

Next topic: about my ease with the shooting of the mob men. The whole killing thing.

I had actually hoped I could just avoid it. Killing anyone, I mean. I'd had many Vacations previous where I was able to either talk my way out of a difficult situation or, as in the case with Constantine, there was always the choice to just "bite the bullet" and let the Earthbound take you out. Pun intended.

It just felt wrong to me; the idea of killing any Earthbound intentionally. Not that other gods have the same squeamishness.

Years ago, I crossed paths with this older god, one clearly at ease with killing. He tried to put it all in perspective for me, although I can't say that I was very receptive to drinking the same KoolAid he did.

It was during a Vacation when I was inhabiting my first police officer. The other god had taken over my Host's partner. I guess it was a mix-up, actually. They don't usually pair two gods on a single Vacation map.

We spotted one another right away. I'd entered my Host in the middle of a shootout and needed to get my bearings. I ended up choosing to hide behind a waste bin until it was over and I could settle in. The other god, meanwhile, shot "the bad guys" with expert ease. After it was all over and we'd exchanged initial god pleasantries, he teased me a bit.

"Not a killer, eh?" He swatted me on the shoulder. "Just as well, best not to start."

"It doesn't bother you?"

"Oh sure, it was very uncomfortable at first, repulsive even. Felt beneath me, you know?"

I nodded. It felt dirty to me too. Something I could never do.

We were sitting in our Hosts' squad car. He began wiping blood off his jacket as he spoke, his voice low, calm, and slightly bored.

"I knew this Earthbound once. I kind of had a crush on her, actually. Hot girl, super smart, super talented. A real action hero, as they say." He chuckled, then pulled a cigarette from his chest pocket.

"I'd taken on a Host who was a hostage negotiator. Senior cop, experienced. His Vacation bio said he always tried to get everyone out alive, was proud of his record as a

negotiator. The other Earthbound, in contrast, also worked for the hostage team, but she was the Marksman — the person that was supposed to wait for the opportunity to end the situation by taking the nut-job out if he wouldn't negotiate or if he started harming hostages." He pulled out his lighter.

"Anyhow, despite my Host and this gal's differing points of view on how to handle such situations, they had this dance, this sort of romantic tension. She seemed normal enough. I could tell she wasn't violent by nature. So I asked her how she ended up in this job. After some boring back history on her life growing up and learning to shot as a hobby with her dad and such, she admitted that it had been really hard at first. The idea of shooting people instead of inert targets, even to protect innocent people, was a challenging proposition. She wasn't sure she could do it, but she took the job."

He chuckled. "Then she said the strangest thing. She told me that over time, it just ended up making sense to her. It became her new normal. She compared the beginning of that routineness of killing to the experience of deciding to wear contacts."

I looked at him, not concealing my frown. "Contacts? What do contacts have to do with killing another Earthbound?"

Having dabbed off, as best he could, the final bits of blood spatter off his jacket, he proceeded to light the cigarette. He took a long drag, then laughed again as he spewed smoke out the window.
"Exactly my reaction. She explained it really simply, however." He took a few more long puffs.

"She said that as a teen, she reached a point when she was tired of the stigma of wearing glasses. So at sixteen, she convinced her parents to get her contacts. The doctor told her to put the contact on the tip of her finger. 'Just touch the surface of your eye, and the contact will cling to it,' he said. She thought he was crazy. Somehow she'd expected there'd be another way to do it. Touch her own eye? Still, she tried it, and sure enough, her eyes began to water like crazy at the first touch. They just poured tears like a river, she said. It was hopeless; she couldn't get the contact in."

Then, he smirked. "But then, she tried again. Over the next few weeks, she did it again and again. She was repulsed but determined, so she persevered. She told me, 'It got just a little bit easier each time, a little bit more familiar.' Her eyes were slowly accepting this new normal. After enough time had passed, she realized she didn't have to think about it anymore; it didn't faze her any longer. She was able to just stab her eye with her finger, and the contact was in. She could just as easily pinch her eye and pull the contact out. No tears."

He turned to look me in the eyes. His borrowed face was stern, his tone serious.

"Killing is like that," he said. "The first time is the hardest; it just feels wrong. But then it gets easier."

"That's why you were smart today, my friend. Best not to start the whole killing thing. Because once you do, there's no going back. It's like smoking — best to just never try it at all. Too addictive, too easy to become habituated." He took another long drag.

Unfortunately, on this Vacation, I forgot his advice, hypocritical or not. No, that's not true; I ignored it. I wanted to stay earthbound longer with Evangeline, so I shot back.

The rest, as they say, is history. It did feel wrong at first, but just like he said, it became easier each time. But I get ahead of myself.

Repulsed yet? No matter, I make no apologies. We all do what we must to get by. We all have our choices to make, even if they don't always look that much like choices at the time.

At least, for this particular Vacation, I can justify my actions as necessary. I'd killed to protect Evangeline, not myself. I stand by that choice.

I'd discovered a protective instinct, and I think I liked it.

* * *

After I'd tidied the suite as best I could, we claimed my rental car and took the I-80 westbound out of New York, heading towards Chicago.

For the first few hours, Evangeline barely spoke. At first, I respected her need to contemplate, but then I couldn't stand it any longer. Plus, I find driving extremely boring.

"So, Evangeline, isn't it time you tell me *why* Constantine's mafia pals are after you? I figure you owe me that much." I'd tried to sound stern.

She stared at me quizzically. "Where'd the patient, 'just wanna help' guy go?"

I immediately felt chided. I don't normally care what Earthbounds think of me, but Evangeline's approval was becoming important to me.

Bother! Even massaging the excuse that I was somewhat put off balance by Evangeline's directness, I also had to acknowledge my desire to please her was growing. Uncertain how the real Adam would act, I had to keep reminding myself that she didn't even *know* Adam before yesterday. It was unlikely she'd become suspicious due to any potential character errors I made.

Still, I couldn't help feeling unsettled and on guard. I was much too smitten to feel comfortable.

She let me off the hook gently. "Can't you guess?"

Keeping my eyes on the road, I shook my head.

Evangeline sighed. "Same old story. I know something I shouldn't know. Something they don't want me to know. Something that could harm their business."

I could feel her gaze upon me, but I kept staring at the road. She seemed bright. How had she ever gotten caught up in this life, I wondered? I waited patiently for her to tell me her plight, to spin her tale.

When she didn't, I peeked at her out of the corner of my eye. She had returned her own eyes to the side window and was staring down at the pavement rushing by, her expression blank. Minutes passed.

I was considering prompting her further when she whispered, "It's so inconsequential, really, that I even know about it. Constantine himself shouldn't have known all the details. It wasn't even his area of responsibility, but he'd heard about it somehow. He was so charismatic, so charming, people just tended to tell him things."

I hadn't found Constantine's memories to indicate anything of the sort, but then again, I'd been in charge of his actions the entire time. I'd never experienced him from a receiving end. While I'd had good access to some basic facts regarding his past business dealings and his underworld life, I admittedly didn't really know how he would normally have behaved or interacted with Evangeline and others before my arrival.

"Unfortunately, he cursed me by deciding to brag to me about what he'd learned," she continued. "It was over dinner, just a couple weeks ago."

This was going nowhere quickly, at least not to my satisfaction. I had no idea what she was talking about. Now that I was in Possession of Adam, I no longer had access to Constantine's Memory Upload, so I couldn't search out the answer there either. Only my growing affection for her kept me from reaching out and shaking her. *Get to the point, Evangeline!*

She continued to muse at her own pace.

"That was a nice night. Constantine was uncharacteristically attentive, complimentary. Considerate even. I didn't know it then, but that would be the last night we spoke. I never heard from him after that." She shivered.

"Then, a few days later, he turned up dead. When I heard he'd been murdered, I wondered what other secrets he'd been keeping that would come back to haunt me."

Evangeline pulled her legs up onto the car seat, pressing her two knees into her chest and wrapping her thin arms around them as though attempting to make herself smaller. Less visible.

"You know, I never planned to have this life," she said softly.

"I was going to be somebody. I was going to rise above my fate, defeat the odds, and reclaim my future, despite the foster care stereotypes, despite the challenges and obstacles. Despite everything."

Evangeline turned to look at me. I knew because I felt her eyes burning on the side of my face, but I kept my face forward and eyes on the road, afraid she'd stop speaking if I met her gaze.

"Despite being a foster child, I was a pretty good kid, apparently, all things considered. Compassionate, helpful; the caregivers in the group homes were always telling me what a joy I was. I don't know what good really was or how I compared to anyone else, I just knew I wanted to fit in, and if unsuccessful, then at least I strived to become as invisible as possible. To survive." Evangeline took a deep breath.

"When I was a kid, I loved to find a corner by myself and read — I taught myself a lot over the years through books." Her voice had grown louder now, more resolute.

"We'd get assigned out of the foster care group homes to families. Paid families. Most of my foster parents were horrid. Luckily, I discovered the gift of the library early and learned I didn't need their help to get books. Books were my salvation, my light at the end of the tunnel. I devoured their secrets, the knowledge and power that those books could give me. They were my escape and my future."

This was the longest, frankest dialogue Evangeline had offered me so far. I bit my tongue again and waited for her to gather her next thought.

"I had plans to go to college, to study law, or something equally important. I knew I could do it if I just pushed myself and worked hard enough. I could make a difference in this world. I could do good."

I took a chance and turned to look at her. Her features had softened as she spoke about her dreams. Then right before my eyes, they suddenly crumbled and twisted again, and I knew her thoughts had shifted back to her current reality.

"Then I met Constantine, and he swept me off my feet. I fell for his savior act, the idea of a fairy tale. I forgot all about my dreams."
Evangeline sighed, letting out a long exhale that carried the weight of too many hurts and secrets, all twisted up together in one big ache too suffocating to ignore.

"When I saw Marcus at the cemetery, I was actually relieved," she said with a sharp chuckle. "Constantine reported to him, and I figured if Marcus was showing his face at the funeral and wasn't looking sideways at me, then maybe I could just fade away and be forgotten. I'd play the cast-aside squeeze, act heartbroken and confused. I would become inconsequential, definitely not worth their time. Cleanup complete."

She began to fiddle with the hem of her un-tucked blouse, where it lay stretched too tight across her bended knees. Her elegant fingers stroked the smooth silk fabric, and the pace of her caress increased with each new word.

"Then Marcus whispered something in my ear, just as they were lowering the casket. I knew then that I was as good as dead."

"What did he say?" I was now completely caught up in her story. I recalled seeing Marcus whispering to her as I arrived. I'd thought he'd been consoling her.

Evangeline turned her face back towards me, and I watched several tears escape to roll down her cheeks.

"No one crosses me or meddles in my business, Eve, and gets away with it. Not even your lousy, sneaky, too smart for his own good boyfriend. He pleaded for his life, right at the end. Then he called out for you. Sorry sap."
I flinched. I'd been there, and I'd done nothing of the sort! Evangeline's name had not only never crossed my lips; it hadn't even crossed my mind. If the Controller had included it somewhere, then I'd completely skipped over that part of Constantine's Memory Upload during those few days of my

Possession. I'd been too busy enjoying the intrigue, relishing the mobster's dance. Too busy to worry about any woman he might have had in his life.

Marcus had lied to her in the cruelest way.

I felt a surge of protectiveness, a desire to punish Marcus. Not for my previous Host Constantine's demise, but for Marcus' misuse of that event to try to scare Evangeline, to hurt her. Our Evangeline. My Evangeline.

"Did Marcus say anything else?"

She nodded. "He said that he knew that Constantine was always trying to impress me, that it showed in Constantine's lack of control of his tongue around me. Then he said, '*He told you things he shouldn't have, didn't he? Too bad for you.*' Then he walked away."

Evangeline wriggled on her seat, squeezing her legs even tighter. Her tone somewhat sheepish, she added, "That's when you and I met."

Another surprise. It dawned on me that she'd known they'd be coming after her, known that they might even decide to kill her. *Well* before we went to lunch.

I'd been manipulated from the very start. Poor Adam! I wondered if he would have fallen so easily under Evangeline's spell as I had.

"You still haven't told me what it is that you know. What secret's worth killing for...."

Evangeline forced a hollow laugh. "Like they need to justify their reasons for killing anyone," she said hoarsely. "I'm just another loose end."

She shrugged. "It's not even that exciting if you ask me. Just a trick of the trade, a method to smuggle drugs into the country. Constantine thought it was so clever, he couldn't resist sharing it with me. He boasted about how it had gone undetected for years. He said they were operating right under the authority's noses, but the Customs Officers were too stupid to figure it out."

She let go of her legs and reached out her hand to touch my arm. "I'd ignored his lifestyle for so long. I tried to pretend to myself that I didn't know what Constantine really did for a living, and until that day, we'd never really discussed it much. When he told me the details of what they were smuggling and selling, though, I was horrified."

She let her arm fall back loosely at her side, then shifted in her seat again, allowing her legs to uncurl back to the car floor.

"I'd as soon forget the whole thing and try to resume some semblance of a normal life, but I guess they're afraid I'll go to the cops."

For a blunt gal, she was taking forever to cough it up. "The secret. The trick of the trade is…."

Evangeline offered me her crooked smile again. "If I told you, then I'd have to kill you," she smirked.

I love puzzles, but I hate mysteries. Yes, there is a difference. Puzzles you choose of your own free will, for amusement. Mysteries are thrust upon you, and often at the worst time. It felt like she was toying with me, poking away at my Achilles heel.

"They found us at the hotel; they know my name. I think I'm already considered your accomplice, Evangeline, so you might as well tell me."

She nodded, her smile waning. "I did drag you into this whole mess without full disclosure, didn't I? I guess I owe you that much. Thank god for your old boys' club loyalty to Constantine."

You're welcome, I thought.

At least she'd bought Adam's excuse for helping her, so my acting couldn't be all *that* bad. Either way, I was along for the ride until Evangeline or Adam's time was up.

Then she explained to me what Constantine had told her.

I have to admit, I found the secret she revealed much more ingenious than she did. Perhaps my lack of experience with this criminal world made it sound more inspired and clever to me than to her more jaded ears.
Or perhaps, my perception was colored by Adam's view of the world.

This whole thing about each Host being unique; it's a double-edged sword. It makes Vacations interesting but also offers an unwanted challenge. Each Host experiences the world through their own filter on perception, in a way. Each one of you inhabits your own mind's unique world. This filter colors not only your opinions and actions but also alters your vision, hearing, and all the other senses; it changes how you actually experience the world compared to others of your kind.

You all pretend to share the same place, but in the end, you can never really know how someone else sees the world, never share their individual interpretation of it. I have a hunch that if you could "see the world through another person's eyes," as you like to put it, that very few of you could bear it.

As a Visitor put in this very position, it can be very unnerving at times. Understanding how the senses work, we gods accept how each of you manages to create your own reality. However, even knowing this, it can be a little unsettling as a Visitor. It takes some getting used to, much like developing sea legs. You Earthbounds don't even see colors the same way from person to person. You have no idea how much trouble I've gotten into during Possessions just trying to grab someone's "red jacket" for them!

Then there's the angles and degrees of attention. Some of you see things in the immediate vicinity clearest. You focus on the closest input. Others are dreamier, always looking at the bigger picture. These ones see the world more like a canvas, always noticing something interesting or out of place in the distance. Some of you feel small, some of you see everything larger than life, including yourself. I could go on and on.

When we gods come down for a Possession, we never know what kind of Host view we'll get. We've learned how to *ignore your vision bias as best we can, these personal mental frameworks you use to travel through your world, but it's an irksome complication at times.*

But I digress. You don't want to know what I see when I take over your body. You want to understand why we gods do it at all. You want to know what I did about it once I decided that you were more than just a place to play, more than just Hosts. I'll get there, but first, there are other things to tell.

Evangeline told me that Constantine's boss had recently refocused his drug smuggling to one of the most dangerous and least understood new drugs, Fentanyl. She shared what she knew about the drug and why it was particularly dangerous. She also claimed the discovery that Constantine was involved with it in any way was what triggered her desire to end things with him.

I had heard about the "Fentanyl epidemic" hitting the States during past Vacations. Fentanyl is opioid-like oxycodone and morphine but 100 times more toxic. The new heroin, it was far more unstable and almost impossible to dose with any accuracy. One pill split in half between two people could have no effect on the first person who ingested it, yet overdose and kill the other.

Apparently, Constantine's boss got involved with it because just a few grams could be used to make 10 kilos of the equivalent of heroin, such that one kilo of the powder could create a million tablets for sale. They were smuggling minuscule bits of Fentanyl hidden inside cell phones.

At least now I understood why Evangeline was a target. Constantine had marked her by sharing what he knew. With less than a day left on my Vacation, I had my work cut out for me if I was going to get Evangeline to safety.

How strange, this pressing desire to help Evangeline at all costs. I normally focused solely on my own Vacation enjoyment, not the mess I might leave behind. I realized I hadn't even thought about my god wager in hours. For the record, my instinct is to argue that I felt partially responsible for the situation she was in since I'd possessed Constantine for what turned out to be his last few days on earth.

However, the more truthful answer, perhaps, is the undeniable fact that Adam and I found her intriguing. And smart in a quirky way. And beautiful.

Ok, the real truth is, Adam had nothing to do with it, clearly. It was I who was drawn to Evangeline. God #201.

Either way, it was nice to feel something for someone beyond myself. Made me feel more…whole. So now I was newly protective and more complete.

I was at war with myself now, torn between two conflicting agendas. What I should really be focusing on was how to win my bet; how to accomplish my goal of controlling outside Earthbounds. And yet….

Perhaps, eternity held some options.

* * *

We had entered the outskirts of Chicago. I took my hand off the wheel to rub Adam's eyes. After over eleven hours of driving, they burned a bit. How I wish we were able to pick and choose which aspects of the living we endured!

I turned onto Hwy 90 and followed it through East Chicago. The motorway was surprisingly light, even for a Sunday afternoon.

Evangeline hadn't spoken in a while. I guessed she was either regretting the decision to share the whole story about Constantine and the drug smuggling or was relieved to get it off her chest but unsure where to go from here.

Whatever the reason, I had a feeling she'd bolt the minute I wasn't looking. She had that cornered animal look about her, that shifty-eyed nervousness that people get when they're trying to look relaxed but are terrified inside. They think their face and body won't betray them, but it always does.

I exited near Grant Park, then turned onto Wacker Drive, following the historic roadway north and then eastward along the Chicago River, heading into the heart of downtown.

I was about to suggest we go to Adam's condo when I felt that animal tingle along my spine again.

Checking the car mirrors, I quickly spotted him.

"What is it? Is something wrong?" Evangeline had noticed my repeated mirror checks and began to turn around in her seat to look at the cars behind us.

"No, don't look back — he might realize we're on to him." I pulled the car quickly in front of a minivan in the fast lane, causing the driver to lay on his horn.
"Who will?"

"Our friend back there. We're being followed. Big tracker-trailer truck, just behind the red Lexus in the outside lane." I began to calculate our options.

"Oh my god! Do you think they traced your rental car? How? Through its GPS system?"

Ignoring her panicked musings, I continued to survey our surroundings, careful to keep other cars between us and the transport truck.

Moments later, I saw my chance. I pulled our car into an abrupt left, swerving onto the North Michigan Avenue Bridge at the last possible moment. I hoped the flow of traffic behind me would prevent the truck from making the same turn.

Evangeline looked over her shoulder, then grasped my arm. "He's slowed, but he managed to cut back across the two lanes and make the turn!"

I frowned. A congestion of cars was blocking our further advancement across the bridge. Apparently, the light traffic was only behind us. I'd miscalculated, and now we were trapped.

I contemplated circumventing the traffic jam by driving the car along the sidewalk, then noticed a short barrier separating the road from the bridge's pedestrian walkway.

While only about two feet high, it was more than enough to rule that escape route out. There'd be no driving over it, and the remaining space between the barrier and the road was too narrow for a car to squeeze through.

Boom!

My body jarred abruptly forward, and I barely avoided cracking my head on the wheel. Evangeline screamed as her own hands slammed into the dash, preventing her from falling forward.

Apparently, the driver of the truck disagreed with my assessment of the pedestrian barrier, for he'd crashed his truck into the back corner of our car. His judgment turned out to be better than mine, as he'd managed to successfully push the front half of our vehicle over the first lower barrier. Our car now straddled the walkway, its undercarriage crunched onto the first barrier, its nose just grazing the top of the second outside wall.

Before I could react, he'd rammed us again. Evangeline's scream was even louder this time. The truck continued to push forward, engine screaming, against the rear driver's side of our car until his own nose was just feet from the outside barrier. The front of our car, meanwhile, had obligingly inched further over the two-foot wall, its underside screeching as parts tore off, no match for the power of the 18 wheeler's engine. As the truck's bumper bore down on the rear of our car, we began to tilt upward slightly, and our car progressed several inches further up the higher outside wall. The driver of the truck was either trying to crush us or planned to force us off the bridge!

We were both flung backward into our seats as the front wheels of our car chose the latter option, rolling further upward against the outer wall's edge.

This wall was much thinner than the first barrier and stood just below shoulder height. Before I could catch my breath, the truck advanced another few inches, sending our car rocketing onto the top of this wall. We were both flung forward in our belts again.

I could hear other drivers honking in panic, their tires screeching as they tried to avoid us and the crazed trucker.

The trucker must have reversed, as he now struck us a third time, inching us further onto our new tightrope stance on the outer wall.

Fate was not smiling on our determined avenger today, however, as our car had become wedged against one of the tall steel flag posts that lined the bridge wall. We held fast, although the front passenger wheel-well immediately began to give way and bend against the thick beam.

While the post was preventing our car from advancing further over the edge, the force of the impact, and the pressure on the wheel and hinges, had caused the front passenger door to fling open.

I began to yell at Evangeline, barking at her to beware of the open door.

"What...?" She had either regressed into that frightened animal state humans seem to favor or couldn't process events quickly enough to be of any use.

Not to be deterred by the troublesome post, the driver of the transport now gunned his engine, urging the truck forward against my side of the car.

The car pivoted against the post, causing the rear to tilt sideways again — angling away from the truck and post, tilting down toward the river below.

Like a lady following her man's lead on the dance floor, Evangeline went with it, her lower body sliding gracefully out the open passenger door. I had no idea such a petite person could scream so loud!

The locked seatbelt tightened heroically across her chest, but it was no contender against gravity, and Evangeline continued to slide further. In seconds, only her chest and face were still visible inside the car.

Then her screams were abruptly cut off as the weight of her dangling body pulled her lower into the tightening belt, and the shoulder strap closed like a noose along her small neck.

She began to claw desperately at the side of the belt, struggling and gasping.

I extended my arm towards her. Her eyes bulging, she took one hand off the belt to reach towards me.

"I'm sorry, Evangeline," I said.

Then I pushed the lock release on her belt.

The strap snapped outwards, and she fell out of the tilted car, plummeting towards the rushing water below. She'd found her voice again – I heard her scream of terror all the way down.

Holding tightly onto my belt's strap, I unlocked it as well.

Releasing my grip, I flung my arms and head forward and dove out the open door after her.

THREE
PAY IT FORWARD

My pointed hands broke the surface first, and then the shock of the cool water and the speed of my entry slammed like a Mack truck across the rest of Adam's body. I felt his chest's desire to collapse but somehow managed to avoid losing the breath I was holding.

As my eyes slowly adjusted to the murky water, my god-luck prevailed, and I spotted Evangeline. She was submerged just a few feet ahead of me.

I began to pull myself through the water towards her, battling Adam's urge to take a breath all the way. I reached her just as I began to feel that I couldn't stay immersed any longer.

Lacing my arm through hers and across her back, I kicked to the surface. We burst into the cool evening air together, Evangeline coughing and gasping, I heaving several deep breaths. I kept a careful grip on her arm as we both took several minutes to recover.

Still struggling for breath, Evangeline pointed to the rocky shoreline along the south side of the river. We'd actually entered the water much closer to the north side, so I shook my head no but then turned and saw that its shore was lined with tall cement walls. South-side it is.

I nodded, and we both began swimming towards the river's edge, kicking and paddling as best we could against the river's flow, which was mercifully moderate this time of year.

When we arrived at the shore, we were greeted by several people who had gathered at its edge, anxiously watching our approach. Several of them helped pull us out of the water, their expressions amazed.

"We saw your car go over the bridge wall!"

"Can't believe you both survived!"

"Are you both alright?"

I frowned at the middle-aged gentleman on my left.

"We're fine, thank you."

I shook off his arm, then reached out and grasped Evangeline's hand. We needed to move. Disappear into the crowd before our hunter on the bridge was able to track us.

Evangeline let go of my hand and reached out to touch the man's arm.

"Thank you for helping us. All of you." She cast her warm, wide smile at the crowd.

"What a fright. Never imagined we'd meet a slumbering trucker in downtown Chicago. Hope he's ok."

Everyone looked back towards the bridge. Her explanation seemed weak at best to me, but they seemed to accept it. I felt proud of her resilience and ingenuity.

"Come on," she whispered. "We need to get out of here. Maybe we can even get some dry clothes somewhere — do you still have your wallet?"

I shook my head. I lost it in the dive into the river.

"No, but don't worry, I have an idea." The curious crowd began to dissipate.

I knew we had more than Constantine's mafia enemies to worry about now. Between the trashed hotel room back in New York and the sunken car, Adam was garnering a lot of his own unwanted attention. I ran through all the possibilities, reviewing Adam's Memory files for anything useful.

"The police are going to investigate our car crash. Before long, they'll trace the rental car to my name, so my condo is definitely out. However...."

I was certain I'd figured out the best option. "I doubt they'll be able to link me to my company corporate holdings. At least not right away. My ad agency has a suite reserved at the Millennium Park Fairmont; it was for one of our out-of-town clients earlier this week. We weren't sure exactly how long he'd be in town; it should still be available. We would be fairly anonymous there, at least for tonight."

In my experience, with the speed the authorities were able to move, we should have enough time to regroup at the hotel and come up with our next steps before they traced us. Like Evangeline, I had no interest in engaging with the earth police. Not while in the middle of a Possession, and not until I figured out the best way to help her. Plus, I didn't have a lot of confidence in any protection the authorities could offer Evangeline, as I feared she'd face her own troubles in their eyes.

Evangeline and I stepped carefully over the rocks and through the bushes that lined the shore. I helped her over the short mesh fence that separated the walkway from the rocks.

We began to walk east along the Chicago Riverwalk, heading toward the stairs leading up to North Columbus Drive. The hotel was just a few blocks south. We should get there before six.

I realized I was famished.

While residing in a Host, not only do we get to enjoy the pleasure of eating, but we also experience their every hunger pang. The Host requires nourishment, regardless of whether or not we are accustomed to desiring it — another one of those Playground pros-cons.

We'd never stopped for lunch, so Eva was probably hungry too, although she hadn't complained all day.

She suddenly struck me in the arm.

"Hey! What's that for?"

She scowled. "That's for dumping me into the river. I thought you were offering me your hand to try to save me, but instead, you cut me loose." Then she shoved me with both hands.

Recovering my balance before I fell, I laughed with surprise. Such a feisty gal!

"Now, wait a minute. You know if we'd stayed in that car we could have died," I protested. "Plus, you were choking. I *was* saving you." I was confident she'd see reason.

Instead, Evangeline continued to glare at me. "Maybe so, but it still felt rotten. You could have warned me or held on to me somehow, or something."

Like there was time!

She was acting irrational, and after I'd just saved her life. Irritated, I clammed up.

We walked together in silence, both leaving a wet print of trailing river water behind us. We pretended not to notice the bemused and curious stares of other pedestrians that we passed. Then I received another Vacation alert.

God #201! A reminder that this Vacation is set to expire in 12 hours. Please confirm receipt.

For some reason, I nervously glanced around.

Calm down! I had become way too jittery on this Vacation. Too many broken rules, I guess.

As I sent up my reply to the Controller, I tried to calm my nerves. I just needed to clear my head a bit. By allowing myself to become so immersed in the life of Adam Juri and his new friend Evangeline, was I losing touch with my true self, my own untouchable existence?

No. Gods cannot be threatened. My true future was limitless. *I will exist forever.* At least, as long as I followed the rules.

My obsession with Evangeline was causing me to forget that this existence within the Vacation was only temporary. It would be of no consequence, in the end. Well, except for the fact that I might lose my bet, although perhaps there would still be opportunities to manipulate a win. My growing concern for her was certainly complicating things.

Regardless, even as Evangeline and I argued, I knew I didn't want this Vacation to end. I couldn't imagine leaving her.

My affection for her was like a virus. I was beginning to feel and act like a nervous, love-sick Earthbound, rather than what I really was, which was just a guest. A supreme guest entranced by a vision, temporarily caught up with a charming host.

A guest whose time here was almost up.

There is a very good reason for "Expirations" on all Vacations to gods Playground.

All visitors to gods Playground must agree to return home within 48 hours.

No exceptions.

Gods will not stay on Earth beyond the Vacation limits, nor return to the same Host on future Vacations, in order to avoid "Identity Confusion." Hosts will be released to their rightful consciousness at the allotted time.

Ah, the unbreakable rule, designed to ensure we gods don't become addicted to earthly life. Yet, for whatever reason, here I was.

I wanted to argue with the Controller. I'd calculated she'd shortchanged my visit by about eight hours. I'd arrived at the funeral in the early afternoon, yet her alerts clearly indicated my Vacation was set to expire tomorrow morning around 6 am. Likely in her haste to squeeze in my extra visit, she'd made an error.

Either way, I was stuck now and didn't dare complain, for fear she'd find evidence of my other rule-breaking activities. And I don't mean just the Body Jumping.

You see, there's another rule I've been ignoring.

Gods will not become attached to Earthbounds.

The rule is actually much longer. I cannot pretend I don't recall it in its entirety since our memory is flawless.

Earthbounds and gods are not equal and cannot form genuine relationships.

All Earthbounds acting as Hosts, and surrounding Earthbound Participants in the Vacation, cannot know about their role in gods Playground.

Earthbounds are creatures that need to feel safe and in control. Earthbound Hosts cannot fear Possession, or they may resist becoming the Host.

Gods will not become attached to Earthbounds.

You get the idea.

I'd gotten myself into a royal mess, with only twelve hours left to do the right thing and leave.

What's that saying you Earthbounds use, "no use crying over spilled milk?" I'd gone down this path with Evangeline, and so far, I had no regrets, even with all the uncharacteristic uneasiness. I felt real for the first time that I could remember.

Yes, I just said, "could remember." I fully realize this contradicts my previous flawless memory statement. But there it is.

I don't like to think about that — that my memory has a starting point, that I can feel the beginning of me. *The beginning of my memories, the sudden onset of being.*

It's unsettling for an all-powerful creature; to consider he wasn't always this way. That perhaps, at some point, he just wasn't there at all.

Until this recount, I've never shared these troublesome thoughts. Not with other gods, not with the Controllers, not with anyone. They tell us we have always existed and that we *will* always exist, and yet….

Gods, with our endless hours spent in empty leisure, are prone to speculating on all sorts of things. The discussion that led to my wager regarding the control of surrounding Earthbounds is just one such example.

There is another common contemplation among my kind, a fantasy, if you will, in which we dream of a "better home." A higher heavenly plane, I guess you'd call it. It only stands to reason that this endless, undemanding, empty state of being cannot be all that lies ahead for us, and so we envision something more. The irony is not lost to me, that we gods dream of a heaven just out of reach.

So we whisper, exchange information, and share our theories. Should this place actually exist, it is rumored to offer a greater, more satisfying level of existence. But how to get there, how to ascend?

I have thought long and hard about this. It is logical to assume that there is more than our home's coffee shop existence, for surely we deserve more, as gods? So I think that, perhaps, it could be that there's some sort of test. I have not yet determined how we must prove ourselves, but I've wondered if we were to demonstrate our superiority, our specialness, could this not be one way to win our place? Perhaps, we can gain entrance to this better realm by establishing proof of our preeminent nature.

It may be that by showing my mastery in controlling Earthbounds, I will ascend to a higher level. Conceivably, winning my wager could pay off in more ways than one.

Yet, the more time I spent with Evangeline, the less focused I became on my bet. Evangeline was becoming more real to me than other gods or the opportunity for new Vacation experiences...but, surely, I wasn't ready to give up on the chance for ascension? If there was a higher plane, I intended to win my admittance for one.

There would be limits to my commitment to help Evangeline;
I must keep focused on my ultimate goal.

"I'd say a penny for your thoughts, but I'm a little strapped for cash at the moment." The sound of Evangeline's voice warmed my borrowed heart, and I gave her a big hug.

"There it is, the Fairmount Millennium Park."

I was grateful for her teasing but chose to ignore her question, as my thoughts were not for sharing.

I ran the last few feet, then pushed through the revolving door. Evangeline followed close behind, catching up to me as I arrived at the Fairmount Gold service desk.

Despite my soggy and aberrant appearance, I needed to convince the concierge to give me access to the company suite. I'd decide the authoritative approach was out. Draping one arm across Evangeline's shoulders, I pretended to topple a bit, then laughed loudly.

"Good evening. What a glorious day we've been having! This is our day to be impulsive before we have to get back to the reality of wedding plans. Please excuse our appearance. My fiancé and I just couldn't resist jumping in the river. She dared me, and I can never say no to her."

I leaned over and gave Evangeline a deep kiss. Luckily for me, she didn't resist. If I'd known for certain she'd play along, I might have tried sooner.

Turning back to the appalled desk clerk, I passed him one of Adam's business cards, which, while soggy, had mercifully survived the river plunge within my pant pocket.

"I'm Adam Juri, CEO of InspiraSource Advertising," I said. "I'm afraid in my haste to entertain my fiancé, I left my wallet in the car. My assistant is just running a quick errand for me, then he'll bring our bags and the car along shortly. I assume he called ahead and alerted you that my fiancé and I will be using the suite we have reserved, likely for a few days." I nuzzled Evangeline's neck.

The clerk's expression was professionally blank. He proceeded to look up the company registration, then begrudgingly handed me back my water-logged card.

"Certainly, Mr. Juri. I see your agency has indeed held a suite for the last few days, and while your corporate guest checked out this morning, it is reserved until the end of the week. Unfortunately, your assistant has not been in touch, so while the room has been cleaned, we don't have your name on file as the next registered guest."

I leaned over the counter until I was much too close to his face.

"No worries, pal! I *am* InspiraSource, so I am registered. Just give us the key, and you can solve the details of your registration records on your own. I think my fiancé and I need to focus on getting some dry clothes."

The desk clerk recoiled a bit, perhaps due to the river smell coming off my clothes, or even more likely, his presumption of my intoxication.

"Certainly, Mr. Juri."

In moments, we had our keys. I turned, dragging Evangeline along with me, making certain to shift us unsteadily on our feet. I pretended to whisper in her ear as we approached the elevators.

Evangeline, while silent, had gone along with my entire charade.

When we were safely inside the elevator, she looked at me with what appeared to be new respect.

"Adam! I would never have pegged you for an actor! Nice job back there. I wasn't certain how you'd convince him to give us a room in our current state, especially without any ID, but you pulled it off rather nicely." She poked my arm, and I swear I saw her blush. "Oh, and you're not a bad kisser, either."

Now I was blushing. I really was becoming too accustomed to inhabiting an Earthbound!

"As soon as we get upstairs, we should order room service. Who knows when we'll get a chance to eat again," I said quickly.

Nodding happily, Evangeline turned to look at herself in the mirrored elevator wall.

"My goodness, I'm a wreck! I don't suppose we could find some new clothes first, then shower and change before we eat?"

I patted Evangeline's arm reassuringly. "I'm sure Adam is listed as having full billing access to the corporate account. Let's pop into one of the shops, and we can bill our purchases to the room."

I pushed the elevator button to send us back down to the lower floor shopping area.

"Adam is listed?" Evangeline pursed her lips, her brow furrowing.

Drat! I'd done it again. Talked about Adam like I wasn't Adam.

"Ha! Battle fatigue." I put on my best embarrassed face. "I mean, you can bill to my account, get whatever you need."

Evangeline continued to stare at me quizzically but said nothing more.

Thankfully, it didn't take her long to find some clothes for both of us in the hotel shops. Anxious to get out of our wet clothes, we re-entered the elevator and rode in silence up to the 36th floor.

Evangeline still hadn't spoken when we entered the room's double doors. The suite was gorgeous, even to my jaded eyes. This time, however, instead of running about exploring or heading off to change, Evangeline surprised me by gravitating to the grand piano that was tucked in the corner by the window.

She slipped onto its bench, then ran one hand silently along the top of the piano's black surface. Next, she lifted the cover, then hovered both hands above the shining keys as though incanting a magical spell long forgotten. After a moment, she gently placed them down and began to play.

I quickly recognized the haunting, classical piece that flowed effortlessly from her small fingers.

I sank into an oversized armchair in the corner, captivated by her surprising talent, my wet clothes forgotten. Her performance of the piece evoked within me feelings of sadness, mystery, and a burning desire, all mixed together in one beautiful, confusing unloading of emotion. I was overwhelmed.

It was a long time since I'd listened to music of any kind, especially music performed with such passion. I'd always been touched by man's ability to create such beauty and magic through music and art — particularly given his undeniable failings and true primitive drives.

Evangeline's piano composition, however, was a tender place to resume my affair with the human arts.

When she was done, Evangeline sat silently, staring out the nearby window at the view of Millennium Park.

"That was beautiful. What was it called?" I asked softly. I already knew the answer, of course, but couldn't think of anything else to say.

She stroked the top of the piano once again, as though it were a living thing.

"Claire de Lune. It's Debussy," she said.

"You play exquisitely. Wherever did you learn to play like that?"

Evangeline gently closed the lid back over the keys, then rose to stroll closer to the window.

Staring out at the setting sun, she placed her hand to the glass as if seeking comfort from the fading rays. "In one of the foster homes, when I was around ten. There was this woman, Caroline, who made our meals. She was so kind, and always looked at you like she really saw you. The inside you. She noticed me poking about the old upright in the living room one day and said if I wanted to learn, she'd teach me."

Evangeline's voice was thick with recalled emotion. "I surprised both of us and picked it up really quickly. Caroline said I was a natural and worked with me every day, right after breakfast was served. She encouraged me, pushed me. She brought me sheet music to practice. We went on that way for almost two years. For a while, I had moments when I could forget about being an orphan, this lost castaway. I felt special. I knew I could make something beautiful with that piano. I had a real talent, something that was mine that no one else had, something that couldn't be taken from me."

Evangeline turned back to face me. She shrugged dismissively, but I could see her pain and truth behind it.

"Then the home became overcrowded, and I was sent to another group home."

"They didn't have a piano. They didn't have a Caroline either. Turns out, the ability to enjoy my new-found talent… it could be taken after all."

She put one hand to her mouth as though intending to pull out the rest of her reluctant words by force.

"I didn't touch another piano for years, never had the opportunity. So I turned to books instead. I only took it up again a few months ago — Constantine found out I used to play and bought me one."

"That was nice of him," I managed.

Her eyes welling up with tears, she nodded. "Yes, it was. He could be thoughtful, on those rare times he thought to make the choice to do so." She gave me her crooked smile.

I wanted to embrace her, to tell her everything would be all right.

"Would you play something else?"

Before Evangeline could respond, however, there was a knock at the door. We both flinched.

I raised my finger to my lips. "Yes? Who is it?"

"Adam? Is that you? It's Caden. Open up, I need to talk to you."

Caden? I scanned the Memory Files Upload.

He had been Adam's right hand at InspiraSource for the last five years. Thirty years old. Loyal colleague and friend. Highly organized, creative, but prone to becoming overwrought if he felt out of control.

Evangeline walked across the foyer, intending to hide in the bedroom. I gestured for her to stay. I was hoping her presence and beauty would distract Caden from any errors I made impersonating Adam.

I opened the suite doors.

"Caden! What a surprise. I was going to call you. It's been quite the adventure, attending my friend's funeral. We just got back into town. How did you find me?"

A tall, thin man stepped into the room.

"Adam! I was so worried when you didn't get in touch these last two days. Why didn't you answer my...?" His voice trailed off as he took in my disheveled appearance and my still sodden suit. Then he noticed Evangeline behind me.

"Oh, I'm sorry. I didn't realize you had company." Caden shifted uncomfortably in his polished shoes, casting a puzzled look between Evangeline and me.

"When the hotel called the agency to confirm the room billing and said you were here, I rushed right over. They didn't mention you weren't alone."

I'd forgotten how we must look. I had to think of something to say. Fast.

Evangeline stepped forward, extending her delicate hand to Caden.

"It's a pleasure to meet you. I'm Evangeline. Constantine's widow."

Then she laughed deeply, her warm charisma filling the room as she dipped her shoulders vulnerably.

"What a sight we must make! Before checking in, Adam and I took a stroll along the River Walk, where we tried to rescue a poor dog that was struggling in the river. I'm a sucker for animals, and Adam's such a gentleman, he went along with my rescue attempt. Anyhow, we managed to save the day but ruined our clothes in the process. Luckily, we purchased a change of clothes. I think I'll go freshen up and leave you two boys to talk."

Without waiting for Caden to have a chance to respond, Evangeline slipped out of the room. Her quick thinking had given me a moment to do some processing of my own.

"Caden, old buddy. Help yourself to some coffee or a drink from the minibar. If you don't mind, I'd like to change into something dryer myself, and then we can talk."

Caden, appearing somewhat more at ease, nodded, mumbled his agreement, then headed over to the bar. I'd caught him frowning slightly as I spoke, however.

Perhaps Adam wouldn't have called him buddy? Was my tone or speaking pattern too varied from Adam's typical way of speaking? When I first began this adventure, when I thought I'd just watch the funeral and leave, I hadn't bothered to playback his voice inside the Memory Files Upload. I'd erroneously assumed that it didn't matter since I hadn't planned to interact with any of Adam's social circle. Given that Evangeline hadn't known the real Adam before yesterday, I'd never gotten around to the typical homework. Yet here I was, jumping into character without a parachute again. I was really off my game this trip!

I quickly ducked into the bedroom. Evangeline was already busy in the bathroom; I could hear her humming away in the shower. Her mood swings continued to amaze me. At least she sounded happier.

I laid out one of the dresses we'd purchased on the bed for her, then selected a new shirt and pants for myself. After slipping into the washroom to rinse my hair in the sink and clean up using a facecloth as best I could, I caught a glance of myself in the mirror. I saw how disheveled I still looked; definitely not in character for Adam. Ah well, the show must go on. I ran my fingers through my hair, quickly got dressed, then went back to the main room.

Caden was sitting on the couch, his back straight, legs firmly crossed, carefully sipping on a beer.

I went to the bar fridge. "I think I'll join you. It's been a crazy few days." I popped open a can for myself.

As I sank into the cushion beside him, Caden put down his drink, then sat back, arms crossed.

"Adam, seriously. What's going on? It's not like you to drop off the radar like that — everyone at the office is a bit worried."

I'd formulated a story in my mind while changing. I just hoped he'd help, based on the version I'd prepared.

"I know. I'm sorry. When I told you I needed to go to an old friend's funeral, I should have told you more about the circumstances and about how long I'd be gone. I'm sure you've been doing a great job holding the fort while I've been away, and I appreciate your efforts in my absence." I paused, then boldly met his gaze. "I'll need you to do that for just a little while longer."

Caden nodded, waiting for more.

"What I didn't tell you is that my childhood friend hasn't led a very honest life these last few years," I began. "Constantine was involved in some less than legal dealings, I'm afraid. When I met his girlfriend at the funeral, the woman Evangeline that you just met, she asked me for my help. Without Constantine, she's at a bit of a loss and is fearful she'll be held accountable for some of his debts and past dealings."

"Past dealings? Are you implying something criminal? Is this girl in trouble with the authorities?" His voice rising, Caden began to stand up.

Grasping his arm and pulling him back down, I dropped my tone to a whisper.

"Shh! She'll hear you. She's innocent, Caden, and naive. It's not what you think. I just need to help her get back on her feet, so she can settle somewhere away from all of the mess that Constantine left behind. That's all. Then I'll be done, and I can come back to work."

Caden shook his head. I'd hoped by sprinkling the truth into my story, he'd accept it. But something wasn't sitting well with him.

"Why you, Adam? Doesn't she have any family? If she's just his girlfriend and not his wife, how can she be held responsible for his business debts? What are you leaving out? This isn't like you."

I started to respond, but Caden cut me off.

"The agency is everything to you. I don't think you've missed a day of work in all the years I've known you. It may have taken years for us to become close, Adam, but I consider us friends. I thought you did too. What have you gotten yourself into with this girl?"

Realizing I may have sounded too dismissive of his concerns, I reminded myself to try to think like an Earthbound, like Adam. Ok…friendship. Loyalty. Those were the themes to tap.

"Of course we're friends, Caden. Good friends. There's no one I trust more. And this friend needs your help right now. I want to help another old friend, to honor his memory by doing this for her, but I can't do that without your help. I need you, Caden."

Caden had sat up straighter again as I spoke, and his lips had tightened into a thin line. I could see in his eyes that I was getting to him, however.

I pressed on. "I want to help her; it's my way of repaying an old debt. It's the final thing I can do for Constantine.

Regardless of how his life turned out, he was a very good friend to me once upon a time. Surely you can understand that." I ran my fingers through my hair, hoping I looked a bit anxious and tired. Actually, I was anxious. Exhuasted. Too much was on the line for me to feel untouchable. I needed him to cooperate.

"Can you get me some cash, Caden? As much as you can. I've lost my wallet, and I don't want to use traceable charge cards right now, anyway."

Caden shook his head again in disbelief but pulled out his wallet. "Traceable cards? I don't understand, Adam. Who's after you? This all sounds like a horrible mistake."

Still, he handed me a pile of folded bills.

"This is all I have on me, just a few hundred. I guess I could go down to the lobby bank machine and get you some more."

Just then, Evangeline emerged from the bedroom. Showered and changed, she was a renewed vision, even without makeup.

"Thank you, Caden. We'll need new IDs, too, since we've both lost ours and likely shouldn't be ourselves anymore anyway. Any ideas?"

Caden sputtered, "Well, I…."

I interjected, "What about your driver's license? I could be you."

When I'd scanned Adam's Memory Upload earlier, I'd noted that Caden had a sister in town. "And your sister's," I added. "For Evangeline."

Caden stood up, then cast his eyes between the two of us, still uncertain.

"My sister's? I'm not sure I could convince her...." When he didn't continue, Evangeline walked over to him, reaching out to grasp his hand gently.

"We really appreciate your help, Caden." I watched her squeeze his hand. "I can see how loyal you are to Adam, how much he trusts you."

She smiled at him again. "We'll mail the licenses back to you as soon as our flight lands." *Flight? Guess she had already planned our next stop.*

I watched as she continued to work Caden. I'd like to claim that at the time, it raised an alarm, made me question who was Evangeline, really? But honestly, I think I was too smitten, too trusting.

She ducked her head, smiling shyly. "I could go with you downstairs to the bank machine, if you don't mind." Then she ran one hand through her flowing hair. "I must be such a sight! I'd like to pick up a few things from the lobby convenience store. Like a brush." She laughed, then grasped his hand tighter and pulled Caden toward the door. He blushed once more.

Wait, what was this? I didn't like the idea of Evangeline alone with him. What if he asked her questions she wasn't prepared to answer?

"Uh, sure. Ok. Have you two eaten recently?" Caden seemed as easily flustered by Evangeline as I'd initially been.

Then I realized what she was really up to. She wanted to ensure Caden didn't take off, didn't talk to anyone. We really did need that cash and IDs.

Grinning at the powers of a charismatic woman, I shook my head. "No. Good idea. I'll order up some dinner for all three of us, and we can all eat and chat more after you two get back."

A little over an hour later, we were all huddled around the room service trolley table. Evangeline had brushed her hair and applied some makeup, and was busily charming Caden. She and I hungrily feasted away as they chatted, while Caden only picked at his plate.

For the first half-hour, Evangeline managed to keep the conversation focused on Adam's ad agency, peppering Caden with questions about our business strategy, core customers, and his and my history.

Caden was obviously passionate about our work and answered her questions enthusiastically. He appeared not only enchanted by Evangeline but also relieved for the distraction that talking about work offered. Over the course of their exchange, he relaxed even further, mirroring Evangeline's warm and upbeat demeanor. I once again marveled at her ability to so readily put anyone at ease, much as she could just as easily put them off-kilter. Depended on her needs, apparently.

Only when dinner was done did Caden broach the subject of our adventure again.

"Ok, you two. I've given you money and my ID, and I'll do my best to convince my sister to give me her ID and bring it back to you by the morning. Adam's never given me a reason not to trust him, but for the record, I don't feel good about all of this. So now, you need to do something for me." He turned to Evangeline.

"Please tell me what you're running from, Evangeline. Is there not a better way to deal with this? Sure, I can cover the office for Adam for another week or so if needed, but are you certain you two aren't getting in over your heads, whatever's going on? Perhaps the authorities could help."

Caden stared at us both expectantly.

"I'm sorry, Caden. You've been so kind, and I can't thank you enough for helping us." Evangeline offered an apologetic smile.

"I'm very grateful for Adam's help, and now yours, but we shouldn't involve you more than we already have. I feel guilty enough as it is about Adam. I hope you can understand."

His body language said he didn't, but Caden nodded.

"I do trust Adam's judgment. His instincts have never been wrong before, and I've learned a lot from him over the years. If he feels he has to do this, I'll support him the best I can."

He paused to look at me, but I didn't know him well enough to read his expression. He turned back to Evangeline. "I hope everything resolves for you quickly."

His brow furrowing, he cast another look my way. "I have to say, Evangeline, that I still can't believe this is Adam." He paused, shaking his head. "I've never known him to be the adventurous type. I just hope you both know what you're doing." Caden continued to stare at me. I wisely kept silent.

Evangeline gave him another big hug. He seemed uncomfortable but returned it stiffly nonetheless. I limited my contact to a pat on the shoulder.

"Alright then, thanks again, Caden. I'll be in touch as soon as I can."

I herded him toward the door. Caden paused on the threshold.

"Call if I can be of more help. *Either of you*. I left my cell number on the pad by the phone. Nice to meet you, Evangeline."

I thought he'd leave, but he pulled me outside into the hall with him.

"Adam, this is so unlike you," he hissed as soon as we were alone. "Are you in love with this girl? I hope you're not getting in over your head."

In love? Sure, I was intrigued by her, off my game around her...I'd certainly broken enough Playground rules already on her behalf. I'd even pondered the notion that my attraction to Evangeline was more than just physical.

But love? In the end, I don't think we gods could actually love anything. Romance is a sweet distraction for the weak, for mortal souls who need to forget their inevitable future. For those who end. Why would I fall in love with something or someone that would one day leave me?

I forced a smile. "Don't worry, I've got my head on straight. I just plan to help her get back on track, and then I'll be back to work before you know it."

Caden shook his head again, staring once more into my eyes. I instinctively averted my gaze. With a final shrug, he patted me on the shoulder and walked into the elevator.

After he'd left, I began to worry. What if he decided I wasn't telling him the truth or chose to tell someone? What if he did his own investigating or stumbled on what we were really running from?

What if Evangeline's mob pursuers figured out we'd been in contact with him? Had we put him in danger? Stepping back into the hotel room, I sank onto the couch.

"There you go again, off to Never Neverland." Evangeline began folding the wings of the room service cart down after first placing the dinner dishes into its center.

"Sorry. Just thinking about what we should do next." I got up to help her tidy up.

Evangeline nodded. We finished in silence, then she pushed the dining service trolley into the hall. I closed and locked the door, then walked back to the couch.

She hesitated by the doorway, choosing to lean against the wall rather than join me on the couch. "Your friend Caden seemed nice. Do you trust him?"

Trust him? I didn't even really know him. The Memory Upload had said Adam trusted him implicitly, however.

"Yes. Yes, I trust him. I wish we could have been more honest with him, though."

Her expression seemed to indicate she wanted me to say something more, so I added, "I don't think he'll mention anything about meeting with us. He'll explain away my absence from work. He'll cover for me."

Evangeline's green eyes narrowed, and she seemed to look right through me.

"When he was leaving, Caden insisted you weren't the adventurous type. Before that, when he and I were downstairs, Caden also made a point of mentioning how out of character you were acting. He seemed genuinely worried about you."

She took a step closer to me, twisting her mouth. "He said you were a workaholic, a straight shooter, ethical in a way that's become unfashionable, but not someone he'd describe as a risk-taker. Other than starting your own business, of course."

When I didn't respond, she just nodded, her face softening into a smile. "He also said how much he admired you but that you were a hard person to get to know." Then her eyes narrowed once again. "He seemed really surprised that you were helping me, a stranger to you."

I was aghast. Now what? Caden had sensed something was wrong, and he obviously didn't really trust me or my story.

Yet he'd still helped Adam.

I felt irritated. Earthbounds were so unpredictable, so emotionally driven. Their motives were always so convoluted and shaded by competing drives.

"Perhaps he doesn't know me as well as he thinks he does. Or perhaps, he knows his place and just did what his senior partner told him to do, out of loyalty. Either way, he should mind his own business and stay out of my affairs."

As soon as I said it, I realized how angry I sounded. How much I probably didn't sound like the real Adam, particularly given that Caden had just helped us out and described Adam as such a saint.

Yup. Evangeline had physically recoiled at my words. I regretted it but wasn't sure how to reset.

Then she straightened, and I knew I was about to be challenged.

Tilting her head, she said, "That's a handsome high horse you have there, Adam."

"Sorry?"

"Do you think you're better than him? Than Caden? Because after meeting you both, I don't. Being the boss doesn't make you special; it just makes you responsible."

I couldn't keep up with her hot and cold reactions to me. She seemed to alter between grateful and sweet, and challenging and judgmental.

Evangeline sat down on the couch. "You know, Adam, I really appreciate everything you've done for me, but I agree with Caden. Perhaps you're too far out of your comfort zone. I still don't know *why* you're helping me."

She turned her eyes away and looked out the far window. "Maybe it would be best if you just loaned me some of that cash, and we parted ways."

Trying to flee again!

"Look, Evangeline, I'm sorry if I offended you somehow. I still want to help you. I don't think you have a choice, anyway. You need me."

Evangeline got up from the couch and walked over to the piano. She slipped sideways onto its bench but didn't open the lid. Instead, she ran her fingers lovingly across the top of the instrument, just as she had earlier.

"Do you believe in God, Adam?"

This had to some sort of Controller trick. Some silly joke. Someone had Possessed her and was making her talk about god. They were trying to mess with me.

Ok, If I'm to be totally honest in this recount, of course, I knew she wasn't actually Possessed (I'd see it in her eyes if she was), but still… where was this coming from?

I didn't know how to respond. No, I don't believe in God, but gods? I was living proof, without the actual living part! *Sorry, did I not mention Adam was temporarily unavailable?* Ha! What to really say without sounding strange.

Reading my silence as reluctance to open up such a discussion, she said, "With the life I've had, you'd probably assume that I don't believe in much of anything. But you'd be wrong."

I really shouldn't have this conversation. Maybe if I remained unresponsive, she'd give up.

"I've always wanted to believe in something. In a higher power." Her eyes reflected off the glistening ebony of the piano top, holding my attention like two dark pools, much too dark to permit a glimpse of their true depths.

Then she surprised me.

"What I really think is that we're all wrong. No one really knows; no one religion has the answer. All the religions have some value, sure, some comfort to offer, but I don't think for one second that any one belief is better than the other."

She smiled softly, as though resigned to a sealed fate. "Whatever form God exists in, perhaps he's frustrated with us. I picture him pitying our confusion and fear, all of our arguing over religion, over our individual desires to be right. He's probably disappointed at our unwillingness to love one another, at our inability to compromise and embrace different visions of his truth."

Now, back home, when I'm away from gods Playground, I'd be the first to admit I'd had a few chuckles at man's expense myself. Until this Vacation, I'd considered humans an entertaining distraction. They are largely driven and controlled by their own fears, by the beliefs they've been taught and subsequently embraced, and by the secret terrors they consume. Their every action, each choice they make, are all driven by these past experiences and misinformed beliefs, and of course, by their animal instincts. Every god knows that humans really are little more than irrational, uncontrolled beasts, wild animals who pretend to be clear thinking, thoughtful beings.

Pretend to be us.

"In the end, it doesn't matter what any of us believe." Evangeline's words began to fall from her lips like single hammer strokes. "Actions matter. Choices matter. Our impact on others matters."

Now what was she saying? For someone claiming not to identify with any one religion, she sure was beginning to preach. Then I surprised myself.

"I believe in supreme beings," I blurted out.

She got up from the piano bench and took a step closer to me.

"So not one God? Do you mean multiple gods, existing at once, like Greek mythology? Or superior life forms?"

Now what? I wished I'd kept my mouth shut.

Then again, maybe Adam was a philosopher. He was entitled to an opinion on God, after all. So I decided to speak about what I knew.

There is the old adage that man is most convincing when speaking from the heart, from his own truth. Of course, the pessimists would argue that there is no one more convincing than a practiced tale spinner, the experienced salesman. A charlatan, preying on the fears and desires of others.

Perhaps, I, god #201, could be both.

"Higher evolved beings," I began, waving my hands. "Creatures that exist in a plane beyond us, that are superior to us. They probably don't even see us humans as sentient in any meaningful way."

I could see I had her attention, and I'd begun to warm to my own soliloquy. "I'd think we'd be more like ants to them," I enthused. "Largely inconsequential, unimportant. Humans are emotional, irrational creatures on the best of days. Yet, in many ways, they are still all alike at the core; all malleable. More like programmable robots than separate beings, particularly if you know how to manipulate them, what buttons to push. When it comes right down to it, people are so basal in their reactions, just another animal trying to survive. More like flailing puppets than true intelligent beings."

Then I realized that Evangeline was staring at me, her revolt palpable.

"Ants? You think that if there is a God, we're just ants or puppets that he can manipulate? That's your world view? How depressing!"

Rats! I wanted her to like Adam, to trust him. I couldn't have her thinking he was a dark atheist.

"No, no, I just meant, if God does exist, we probably aren't on his radar. We're not evolved enough. Not important enough. He'd be more powerful than us, exist above our understanding."

Evangeline shook her head vehemently, then turned away from me and began to pace before the room's large window.

"No, I disagree. There's something out there, something bigger and more important than us, sure, maybe so, but something that still cares, that still believes in us. That is a part of us. I have to think that someone or something is watching over us, hoping we choose to nurture the best parts of ourselves rather than fall into the dark."

Evangeline rested her forehead on the glass of the suite's window.

"I refuse to believe this is all an accident, without purpose. Perhaps it is a place for us to learn about ourselves, to find our path to a higher existence." She gazed out at the view of the city skyline and gardens below.

Then she spun around and took two long strides towards me. Sitting down beside me on the couch once again, she leaned in closer.

"What I know, what I believe, is that what each one of us chooses to do *matters*. Our impact on others, our actions and choices, they *matter*. If nothing else, it's about our legacy, our impact on the world. The mark we make."

Leaning back now, her voice shook with passion. "Despite what you might think, despite my relationship with Constantine, I've always tried to live my life so that when I die, I can have no regrets, so I can be proud of who I was. I want to do *good* in the world, even if that is only possible through the day to day caring and respectful treatment of other people. Even if I never achieve a position of power or influence, I can still impact the people I interact with each day through my actions and words. Through small acts of kindness, acts of consideration." She grasped my hand. "The whole 'pay it forward' idea, you know?"

She was staring at me, her eyes wide and hopeful, waiting for affirmation of her chosen belief.

I felt sorry for her. I realized that I also had never felt so helpless.

"People are selfish creatures," I retorted. "Motived by self-preservation, self-interests, and the desire to protect and further their own survival and advancement. They don't deserve your respect, or your caring. At best, 'pay it forward' is a fad. Like so many other do-gooder ideas, it will pass."

I was speaking without thinking again. Losing my perspective and allowing my own sour thoughts to spill uncensored to this woman. Perhaps the Controller was right, and staying Earthbound too long was unhealthy.

Her smile drooped, and her eyes lost their sparkle. "I'm sorry, Adam. I guess we're too different." She sighed. "How sad for you, to believe in nothing."

She seemed to ponder something, for she fell silent for a moment before stating softly, "Yet you've chosen to help me."

She got up once again and walked over to the kitchenette. Opening the fridge, she grabbed a bottle and proceeded to pour herself a glass of Perrier. After several moments of silence, she spoke without making eye contact with me.

"What you or I believe, or don't believe, doesn't matter. We should just be good anyway, do good anyway. Show compassion for others whenever we can. Because we can."

She was still not looking at me. After a long pause, she added, "I think God gave us life. In one way, you might be right; he's not going to save us. It's up to us to save ourselves. We can show our gratitude for his gift by not wasting it, but not tarnishing it. By conducting ourselves in a way that is worthy of God's gift. We need to make the right choices, the good choices."

Now Evangeline did look at me. Her tight smile was made more of pity than warmth.

"I believe we're all here to learn something. There are lessons we need to figure out, things that need to be taught to us while we're here. Learning to be good, that's just one of them. Recognizing the dark and avoiding its pull, that's another." She sighed once again.

"At least that's the hope, the belief, that keeps me going. It lets me sleep at night, even on the darkest of days." She raised her glass. "To the purpose of life, and paying it forward. Cheers."

I'd been rightfully dismissed.

Evangeline unsettled me more than any other human interaction ever had in all my memory. She made me question myself.

I decided I didn't like it. She was ruining my Vacation.

"Look, I said I'd help you, and I will. While I'm certainly no guardian angel, I don't break my promises."

She seemed unimpressed. Trying to catch her eye, I added, "For the record, I'm not against doing a good deed, as my efforts on your behalf attest. While the only lesson life has ever taught me is survival of the fittest, I'm still not depressed, nor cruel. I can be a good person without believing in your God. I said I'd help you, and I will. In deference to Constantine, a good friend who died too young at the feet of his own bad choices. That being said, if you still want to part ways, that's fine with me too." After this last lie, I stood up, intending to storm off into the other room.

I didn't. For despite everything, I realized I really didn't want to be mad at her, didn't want to leave.

I was still drawn to her and found her fascinating, albeit also irksome and frustrating. I just wanted control over my own holiday, that's all, and she was messing with that. Ah, what's that saying about aging love? The bloom was off the rose.

Evangeline walked around the kitchen island and moved towards me. Putting her glass down on the coffee table, she abruptly reached out and smothered me in a huge embrace.

She smelled like flowers and soap, and it felt as if small electric shocks were jumping from her body to mine. She oozed life and hope. I wanted to keep seeing her as a sneaky vixen, but I knew it was a lie. She really was an earth angel, someone unique. Someone kind and pure of heart.

It was hopeless. I would never have control over this Vacation. Such is life.

I fell back in love.

She placed her cheek next to mine, and her warm breath caressed my ear as she whispered, "I believe there's hope for you yet, Adam Juri. You may yet avoid the sentence of eternal hell before your time is up and judgement is upon you."

I must confess she'd caught me off guard again with that one. I flinched at her words and leaned back, thereby caused us both to tumble backward together onto the couch.

She landed on top of me with a slight squeal, which she immediately followed with a hearty laugh.

"So, you *do* believe in something, even if it is just eternal damnation," she teased, in no rush to release me, apparently.

Then she smirked. "Perhaps it is *I* who will teach *you* something." She continued to smile at me.

I believed nothing of the sort. Certainly, I didn't believe in damnation. She'd just surprised me with that cryptic comment about my time being up. Of course, she couldn't possibly know who or what I really was, but since my time *was* running out on earth, at least for this Vacation round, her comment had hit home.

It was after 11 pm now, so by my calculation, I had seven hours left before the Controller told me to come back up. My time with Evangeline was almost done.

Evangeline interrupted my thoughts as she disentangled herself from me and got back on her feet. "Let's get some sleep, and then we can get on the move again bright and early tomorrow. I was thinking New Orleans."

I nodded and waved her off to the bedroom. With only a few hours left before my Vacation expired, I needed to figure something out before morning.

Well, to be perfectly honest, I'd already decided I wasn't going home. Not yet. I couldn't leave her until I knew she was safe.

Think! Once I missed the Callback time, there would be consequences. Significant consequences. Things would happen that I couldn't hide from Evangeline, things that would be impossible to explain.

Then it hit me.

There was one way to keep my secret from Evangeline and yet still outwit the god Police.

A way for me to stay beyond the set Callback time, to avoid leaving gods Playground, and yet still not tell Evangeline who I really was.

It was simple, really. I don't know why I hadn't thought of it earlier. I just needed to make Adam untraceable by the Controller and her god Police.

If I wanted to stay and protect Evangeline, I would have to kill someone.

I had to kill Adam.

FOUR

TRACING POSSESSION

So here's the rub.

Earthbounds rarely resist Possession. Basically, you can't fight something you're unaware is happening. The Controller regularly reminds Visitors to gods Playground that it's critical that Earthbounds never learn of our existence, or perhaps, more truthfully, our interference in theirs.

Such knowledge on behalf of the Earthbounds could be catastrophic to our future abilities to enjoy our favorite escape. Should Earthbounds learn of our place in their lives, then likely many of them would quickly learn how to feel that tickle in their brain, that invading presence. Soon after, they would begin to discover how to resist us and likely tell others.

Even the simplest of you Earthbounds could repel or fight Possession if you actually understood what was happening to you at the time. A few of you have stumbled on this already, even without understanding what is really going on.

Now, with all of us Vacationing visitors spread about the earth, you might also wonder how we gods recognize each other. As I mentioned earlier, it's all in the eyes. Just as I can Body Jump by making eye contact and concentrating, similarly, if I look into a body's eyes, I can tell if the original soul is in Possession or if a god has taken over.

The Controller traces human Hosts in a similar way. She tracks humans, tracing their body's location by their essence

121

— that same original "soul" signature that shines through their eyes. She can trace their location anywhere on earth by that unique human autograph, that presence of the Earthbound's spirit that glows from within.

You humans are actually aware of this to a limited extent. When a spirit is fading or lost, you see it in their eyes. At the very least, you recognize it at a subconscious level. That vacant stare, that lack of presence: you instinctively recoil from it, you sense it and are afraid. Sometimes you see it as madness or illness, which I guess, in a way, is accurate. When a particular Earthbound's soul is dying or has begun to leave, you recognize the death churn in their eyes. You instinctively see how their soul twists and cries.

So now you know how we find you, how we find our chosen Hosts. Human signatures are easily traced by the Controller, and no Earthbound can hide from her. She simply picks one and places us in their physical home.

This brings us back to my plan.

My time on Earth would be up soon. Normally, when our forty-eight hours are up, we gods simply release the Host body back to the original owner. Back to the Earthbound.

We've been told that none of us gods have ever overstayed our welcome. No one before me has dared to miss the Callback, dared to break the Vacation Expiration rule of gods Playground. At least, that is the party line.

That being said, all of us gods are well aware of the existence of the god Police. In theory, any half-present mind would realize that their very existence, these lurking god

Police of legend, would, of course, thereby suggest that other gods may have breached protocol in the past. Someone must have disobeyed, must have broken the rules before. Why would the god Police exist otherwise? One must also consider that there are gods that were suddenly no longer among us — those who disappeared.

What is known is that should one ever choose to overstay the forty-eight-hour Vacation allotment, the god Police, along with the Controller's help, would simply trace the location of the Host body through its original soul and then come down to reclaim the fugitive god.

Since they can locate any human soul's location at any moment in time, there really is no hope of hiding. So no point trying to extend your Vacation, even if brave enough to face the consequences.

Unless....

It occurred to me that I could eject Adam. If I were to wrest Adam himself from his body, if I could displace his soul, then the remains would technically become mine alone. They would be untraceable. There would be no signature, nothing for the Controller to follow.

There is no tracking system for us gods. I have a hunch this is not because we are special or all-powerful. My guess is that, most likely, it has just never come up. The necessity to trace ourselves has never been realized. Or perhaps, if we are truly untraceable, then it is only by accident, by pure luck or a lack of knowledge, rather than any extraordinary power we hold within ourselves.

Either way, at the time I made my decision to stay on earth, I had no choice. If I wished to remain beyond the Vacation allotment, I needed to change Adam. Permanently. I needed to truly take over his body for my own.

I needed to make him like a god. Make him all-powerful. Make him untraceable. Make him me.

I must brag now. To my knowledge, this has never been attempted, never been done. At least, not in any recorded way. Based on the efforts that arose to reclaim me, I believe that no one had done this before me. Wisely, no one else ever will again, I'd wager, given how things ended. As you'll see, it didn't turn out so well for me, this brazen decision to defy the powers above.

Please don't think too highly of me or my bravery. I prefer to remain unsympathetic, perhaps pitied at best. Let your judgment be harsh, given what we gods have done to your kind. It seems only fair.

Or perhaps, I protest too much, and you hate me already.

Honestly, I wasn't really rash, nor brave, nor confident. I just knew I had to try. For Evangeline. She needed me, and I needed her. Adam had to go so that I could stay.

What happened next was most unexpected, but not, perhaps, without forewarning.

In retrospect, I have a sneaking suspicion that I knew the danger all along, even sensed something special about Evangeline. However, I managed to convince myself that it was not real nor important. At the time I decided to kill

Adam, I just wanted to stay a little longer. It's as simple as that.

Perhaps I'd already become too human, too caught up in my emotions to function rationally. I was a victim of a classic case of Identity Confusion. While my affection for Evangeline was most certainly just a fabrication of my imagination or a side effect of my Vacation euphoria, I am still accountable for succumbing to it, nevertheless.

So, judge my actions before and after the subsequent events as you may, for I will offer no further apologies.

If it helps, I eventually decided to care for more than just Evangeline. I decided to care for the future of all of you. For all you Earthbounds.

Perhaps, if I'm to be truly honest, it wasn't a Vacation fantasy, and I truly loved her after all. Why would I have taken pity on all of you if not for her?

But I've gotten ahead of myself again. First, I must tell you how I killed Adam.

*   *   *

Evangeline was fast asleep. It was around midnight, and time was running away from me. In less than six hours, the Controller would expect me to return, and she wasn't known for her flexibility. At least, not around Vacation end times.

I had committed to the idea of murdering Adam. To be honest, or perhaps in my defense, I wasn't entirely certain what would happen to him once I managed to wrest permanent control of his body away from him. I just knew that I was determined to eject his presence from our shared home, to claim it for me and me alone.

That's the harsh truth; gods don't worry about where you Hosts all go when you die — it remains a mystery. We don't know what happens to you after death, and honestly, none of us care to know. Sorry to break it to you — I've never run into any of you back home. I realize I'm not winning any points for telling you this, but to all of us gods, you're just Hosts, just places we stay for a short while until we move on to another.

As for me (while there would come a time when this view changed), on that night in the hotel, the night I decided to kill Adam, I was still just like all the others. I was simply working on the logistics of securing my place on Earth.

I had two problems to solve, I reasoned.

First, I needed to wake up the real Adam in order to be able to actually force him out. Secondly, I needed to figure out how to kill Adam, but in such a way that I could still bring his body back for myself.

I'd had what I considered a clever idea, one that could solve my second problem. While there were a lot of things that would need to happen at just the right instant in order for me to pull it off, I was reasonably confident that I could manage the intricacies of my plan and eject Adam for good. The only gamble was finding a suitable second Host before my time ran out, to act as my bridge.

However, before I could put my brilliant plan into action, I first needed to figure out how to wake Adam.

When we gods take Possession, you go into a dream state. Your essence "sleeps." If I was going to force Adam to leave, I needed to wake him up; so we could fight for what we both believed should be ours.

We gods are used to the task of quickly suppressing you, of forcing Hosts into a dream state. I admit, at that time, I wasn't really certain how best to bring Adam out of it. Waking you up just wasn't normally on our agenda. We usually just release the body when we leave, and then the Suppression stops.

This time, I wanted him to leave instead of me. Yet there was no hope of ejecting him without his alertness. Sleep has a strange way of protecting your mind's presence. Your essence goes deep during sleep and isn't open to outside influences like the awakened mind. We gods can't even take Possession while you're sleeping. In order for us to take over a Host, you need to be awake, then suppressed back into a dream state once we're inside, as strange as that sounds.

I must have fretted on this for over an hour, and then the final piece of the puzzle came to me.

Everyone knows that outside physical influences can shock people awake. Visiting gods are reminded that while in Possession of a Host, there is the risk that they might return to the surface through some outside trigger. Loud sounds, unpleasant or sudden changes in temperature, or even pain, are all physical effects that can cause a human Host to awaken. When Constantine and I were shot, he began to resurface just before our death. The pain woke him up.

My plot to take control of Adam's body permanently was now complete.

After ensuring that Evangeline was still fast asleep, I quietly let myself out of our hotel room and began searching the hallway. Within minutes, my search was rewarded.

I spotted the bright red box hanging on the wall just a few doors down from our room. AED's (Automated External Defibrillators) were placed in most public gathering places these days, and I recalled seeing several throughout this hotel.

I examined the device and was relieved to see that it was the semi-automated version. Even better, it had a manual override button. Luck was on my side tonight.

Glancing quickly down the hall in both directions to ensure I was alone, I opened the case and removed the defibrillator box. After placing it carefully on the floor, I took off my shirt, which I then hung on the open case door.

Squatting down, I began to examine the defibrillator device more closely. I could see it had the typical layout. Satisfied I was ready, I flipped the On switch.

The defibrillator began to hum as it powered up. I lifted the lid and removed the two patch paddles that were attached by long cords to the main power box.

"Attach pads," a smooth, automated female voice said.

I jumped. I guess I was a little nervous. I'd forgotten that all of these devices had a built-in Voice Command Guide. Nodding like a schoolboy, I peeled the backing off each pad and stuck one on my collarbone just above my heart and the other alongside my breastbone on the opposite side of my ribcage, just as the pad image indicated.

"Do not touch patient. Analyzing heart rhythm."

I decided I didn't like her. With that overly calm yet still cheerful tone, she reminded me of the Controller. Undeniably knowledgeable, sure, but my gut instinctively struggled to give her my complete trust.

I frowned, waiting for her to run her course.

Now, I'm guessing many of you have a misguided understanding of how defibrillators really work, likely from watching fabricated medical dramas on television. Having been in the presence of true medical personal on past Vacations, I knew the actual facts.

A defibrillator cannot restart a heart that has completely stopped beating. Only CPR and certain drugs can do that, such as vasopressors like epinephrine. When you see a flatlined patient given a defibrillating shock on television, it's a lie. It wouldn't work. It couldn't bring them back.

Defibrillators are actually used to shock a human heart out of a bad cycle. They terminate a bad rhythm. Specifically, they're intended to interrupt life-threatening cardiac dysrhythmias and ventricle fibrillation; to terminate a heart attack or cardiac arrest rhythms. Defibrillators should be used on individuals that still have some heart activity, albeit abnormal.

The defibrillator administers an electrical shock that depolarizes the heart muscle, thereby terminating the abnormal rhythm. *It stops the heart, not starts it.* I believe the medical term for the resulting state is "asystole," or what is more commonly called flatline.

This stoppage is intended to break the heart out of its current abnormal cycle. The shock administered by the defibrillator causes the heart's muscle cells to contract simultaneously, interrupting the spasm or dangerous rhythm. Then, if all goes well, the heart will restart and reestablish a normal sinus rhythm through its own natural pacemaker. Although not always successful, the theory is that the heart will naturally "reboot" and return to a normal rhythm. It does happen. People save the day.

This means administering a defibrillator shock to a normal, *healthy* beating heart is a very bad idea.

The device's electrical shock would effectively interrupt the healthy heart rhythm and stop it from beating.

So now you have a good idea of my plan.

I was going to wake Adam up, then quickly shock us, thereby stopping our heart. We'd be ejected before he ever clued in. He could leave, and then I could return.

I just needed a little help, a little insurance, to make sure his heart restarted once I'd gotten rid of him. I'd deduced that I needed to Body Jump out of Adam at the moment of the shock and remain outside just until I was certain he was dead and gone. Then I could return to his empty Host through a second Jump, and I'd have won. I'd become Adam, human god, untraceable one. *Sorry Controller!*

The defibrillator had finished her analysis of Adam's heart rhythm. "Shock not advised," she said sternly.

I chuckled. "Sorry, Hun, but I disagree."

I sat, crouched on the floor, waiting anxiously. Luck also disagreed, for within minutes, a shadow began to form on the opposite wall.

A rotund figure began to round the corner, his thick midline bulging out of the loosely tied belt of his hotel bathrobe. Beefy, bare toes poked out of the front of black hotel slippers, and an empty ice bucket swung in one large hand.

He didn't notice me at first, for his balding head was buried within his cell phone.

If this was going to work, I needed him to notice me, to make eye contact. I also needed to wake Adam up, a.s.a.p.

I stood up and threw Adam's body into the wall, ensuring his shoulder struck the defibrillator box that hung there. I winced as the shock of the impact rippled through his body.

Apparently not in a compliant state, Adam remained suppressed, holding on to his dream state. I was still alone in here.

My friend down the hall had looked up at the sound of my body striking the wall, however. His expression was one of fatigue and mild confusion.

"Help, help!" I cried out quickly, determined to carry out my plan. "I think I'm having a heart attack!"

I looked about for something else to awaken Adam. Grimacing in anticipation, I reached out and placing my left hand inside the wall's defibrillator case. Grasping the case's door with my right hand, I swung it shut as hard as I could on my other hand.

Yikes!

That did it. Adam's essence awoke with a start, and it was all I could do to subdue his yelp of pain. The hand hurt like hell, but I was fairly certain I'd only bruised it and not broken anything.

Then I experienced the strangest sensation yet, as Adam tried to take over and began speaking. I had to fight the urge to suppress Adam back into sub-consciousness.

What the hell…." Adam regained his balance shakily and took one stumbled step forward, staring about in confusion.

Adam, it's time for you to go.

I tried to speak and discovered Adam's lips felt like mush, like putty that had to be molded, rather than flesh or muscle.

"Help me," I slurred, beginning to panic now as, for the first time, I wondered if I could really pull this off.

The bathrobe man took one hesitant step towards us, although it was clear he was frightened by Adam's behavior.

"I'm having a heart attack," I said, although the words sounded garbled to me. Real Adam raised one hand to his lips as though batting away my words. I had better control of the eyes, however, and managed to lock gazes with my reluctant witness.

Without breaking eye contact, I attempted to force Adam to reach out to the defibrillator. After several frightening moments of struggle, we fumbled around until I was able to direct his hand to the bottom right of the box face, where I'd noted the Override shock button was located. I pushed it.

"Charging, stand clear," my automated girlfriend intoned cheerfully.

I felt Adam's eyes widen and realized with horror that he was trying to look away from our obese friend. He was trying to look down at the defibrillator device.

"What's happening?" Adam spoke again, and I struggled to keep his eyes locked on our hallway friend.

"Press flashing shock button now," continued the defibrillator Voice Guide. "Then stand clear."

I felt as if Adam's eyes were about to bulge out of his head, and both eyes began to water as I fought to keep contact with bathrobe man. Adam and I continued to wrestle for control of his body for what felt like minutes. His right arm began to jerk left and right, spasmodically making its way back to the machine waiting on the floor.

Push it!

I managed to twist a half sneer, half smile, across Adam's face, as our right hand finally found our flashing friend. *Triumph!*

As I depressed the Shock button, I had an instant of doubt. Ignoring the instinct, I prepared to initiate a Body Jump to my hallway friend.

Then Adam's face went slack, and I felt our eyelids begin to flutter before I could leave.

As over 1000 volts of electricity raced through the electrodes within the two patches on our bare chest, I realized with surprise that it felt nothing like the moment of death by Constantine's bullet.

The electricity at first felt like that sensation you get the instant you awaken from a bad dream. Like that startle of returning to yourself and to alertness. That jolt of, "I'm still here!"

Then there was a feeling of immense stiffness and tightness throughout the body, as though every muscle fiber was trying to extend and contract at the same moment. It felt like one massive muscle cramp.

I was distracted by this difference but somehow managed to open a slit in our eyelids. I had to get out before our heart stopped. Bathrobe buddy! He was staring at me, his jaw slack, ice bucket tumbling to the floor. Eye contact – Jump!

White light, followed by relief. I was now inside the heavy-set bathrobe man. His frightened, nervous breathing filled the air around me like a foghorn, and he was sweating profusely. As I struggled to see clearly, I realized that he must normally wear eyeglasses. Likely he'd not bothered to put them on for his brief voyage to the ice machine.

I quickly suppressed my new Host and then walked him over to Adam. Adam lay slumped on the floor, his upper body draped backward across the side of the defibrillator, one arm tucked awkwardly underneath him (the arm we'd struggled over while trying to push/not push the shock button).

Kneeling down beside my past Host, I placed a finger alongside his throat, checking for a pulse.

Adam was definitely gone. His sinus node, as expected, hadn't restarted his heart. The misuse of the defibrillator had resulted in a more permanent asystole state.

He was dead.

My defibrillator gal pal wasn't ready to be ignored. She was focused on her own agenda. "Shock one delivered," she said smoothly in her calm voice. She was really riding my last nerve. "It is now safe to touch the patient. Commence CPR now."

"Brilliant idea, sweetheart," I said, then cringed as I heard my new Host's husky smoker's voice.

I knelt down beside Adam's lifeless body and pulled him over until he was flat on the floor. I began chest compressions, looking up and down the hall as I did so, keeping an eye out for any unwanted guests. The defibrillator helpfully began to emit repeated paced dings, helping to time my compressions. After a bit, she said, "Give two breaths to patient now. Breathe."

I complied.

"Stop CPR. Stop now. Do not touch patient. Analyzing for heart rhythm."

I waited, then once again, looked anxiously up and down the hall. I needed to get back into Adam pronto.

Why was his heart taking so long to restart? I'd delivered perfectly executed CPR, and he was still a young man. Why was his body not responding?

As seconds ticked by and I continued CPR, I began to panic. This really was taking too long. What was the number of minutes until brain damage was it one or two? I needed his body to function normally when I returned. It would be useless to me if he turned into a vegetable.

I glanced down at my current Host's bulging frame and shuddered. If I couldn't get back into Adam *right now*, I was going to have to consider other options. I sure as hell wasn't staying in here.

Then Adam's body gasped, as his first breath in minutes shuddered through his chest.

I leaned in close to his face, my new Host's borrowed heart racing with anticipation.

Adam didn't open his eyes.

He didn't open his eyes.

Shit, shit, shit! What had I done?

Adam, the real Adam, had left, gone wherever the hell you all go when you die. Now all that was left was this vegetable, this comatose body that couldn't open its eyes.

Open your eyes!

How was I going to Body Jump back into Adam if he wasn't there to help me? Now real panic set in. I'd miscalculated, and it was going to cost me. I'd really screwed up!

In a last move of desperation, I reached out and peeled back Adam's eyelids with both hands. Leaning in close to stare into his vacant eyes, I hissed, "Let me in, dammit. Evangeline needs me. She needs us."

Adam's lifeless body starred emptily back at me, like a lover who's lost all interest and is just waiting for you to realize they've stopped caring about you. Waiting for you to leave.

I shook him violently, then began pounding on his chest angrily. He'd let me down, just when I needed him most. I peeled his eyelids open again, just so that I could glare at him.

Then it happened — that flash of light, the feeling of surging forward.

I was in, after all.

It was different this time, different than it had ever been before. But I was in.

Adam's body lurched forward, and I emitted several strangled gasps as I sat my new/returned body up.

Meanwhile, my abandoned temporary Host, bathrobe man, was also slowly righting himself. Rising to his feet beside Adam's body, he shook his head as though clearing a bad dream.

"What…?"

Pushing my body to a sitting position, I quickly struggled to my feet and reached out to embrace bathrobe Host.

"You saved my life!" I said with as much exuberance as I could. I could see he wasn't convinced, so I continued to hug him, followed by a warm kiss on the cheek.

"God bless you! You're my hero. I thought for sure I'd die of that heart attack, but you saved me."

Bathrobe man gave me a confused, uncertain look, then cast his gaze up and down the hall.

Jason! Jason, please!

Confused myself, I looked around, uncertain where the call had come from.

Deciding I'd misheard, I quickly refocused on bathroom man. "Of course, you're in shock too. Thank you, thank you," I gushed, determined to complete this scenario and get back to the room. Back to Evangeline.

Bathrobe man's eyes cleared as he focused on my face. A huge, albeit perplexed smile, broke widely across his fleshy face.

"You're welcome." Then he smothered me in a huge hug, his robust arms encircling me like a python's death embrace.

Gently pushing him away, I wriggled out of his embrace. "You're a true hero. I wish I could stay and chat, but I need to get back to my wife. God bless."

Before he could engage me further, I dashed down the hall, pulling the room key from my pocket. I didn't look back to see what he did. Let his weak mind sort out its own lies. Missing moments of memory or not, I was confident he'd come to terms with it.

Denial is a human specialty, after all, as well as the secret to your sanity.

* * *

Investigative Report by god Policeman #632
re Protocol Breaches: Body Jumping Incident #2
& Murder of a Host, Incident #1

– Offending god #201

As indicated in my previous report, #201 repeatedly broke gods Playground rules and utilized Body Jumping to further his own interests. Part of his rehabilitation will be to suppress the knowledge of this mode of travel below his active operating memory. The situation will be resolved to the Controller's satisfaction before releasing #201 for further circulation and Vacations.

Of greater concern was the revelation that #201's had attempted to avoid detection and prevented further observation by the Controller through the murder of Host Adam Juri. This action was not discovered until after his recovery and will be dealt with in a separate trial.

Further, as this action was a unique occurrence within gods Playground, this officer has no further recommendations at this time, pending a full review of all applicable Playground protocols and laws. Additional charges are likely pending once the full results of #201's actions are recorded and understood.

(Resumption of #201 narrative)

* * *

My temporary Host already forgotten, I entered the room. I was relieved to see Evangeline was still asleep.

I walked over to the hotel bar and pulled a mini bottle of rum from the fridge, draining it in one gulp. I'd seen so many Hosts do this to settle their nerves, I'd figure as a new "full-bodied human," I'd give it a try. Not the most rational action, but let's face it, I'd given up my superior mental control days ago. Next, I plunged my bruised hand into the ice bucket (kindly filled by the maid when we arrived).

I felt sleepy, strange, and disorientated. I'd never been in control of an abandoned body before, and it was a surreal experience.

The body seemed heavier. I felt more earthbound, if you pardon the lame witticism. While my Possession was now a solo act, and I certainly felt more in charge without the Controller's looming contact, it also felt more cumbersome. Uncomfortable. Like that feeling of grabbing what you thought was your own coat, then getting that itch when you realize you've actually put on someone else's jacket. Even if it looked identical to yours, you feel the difference because you weren't the one who originally broke it in.

I decided I didn't like the feeling.

Regardless, I'd have to put up with it for now, at least until I was sure Evangeline was safe. She trusted Adam, and this body would now ensure that I could stay here without being traced. But I couldn't inhabit the dead Adam forever. Something was off. It felt wrong, and every instinct told me not to prolong this new state.

I was also exhausted. Apparently, even without the Host, the body still required rest.

There were still a few hours until dawn. I decided to try to sleep. I closed my eyes and lay back on the couch. It took me a few minutes to figure it out — how to fall asleep without a Host to pull me in. Eventually, I was able to shut out my surroundings, and my mind drifted off into sleep.

A bright corner office, high above the city. Furnished with a mahogany desk, leather chairs, and a large collection of glass sculptures. I was standing by the wall of glass, smoking.

As I stared out the window at the cityscape, I heard the office door open behind me.

"Excuse me, sir. You have a visitor."

I was in no mood for unsolicited company. After taking another puff of my cigarette, I spun around, intending to wave my assistant off. Then I saw the woman standing behind her and nodded instead.

Rachel entered the room, her long, amber hair glowing softly under the morning sunlight that streamed in through the glass behind me. Her face, ordinarily bright and youthful, was pinched and grey with exhaustion, uncharacteristically betraying all of her 31 years.

"Jason. Thanks for seeing me." She hesitated on the threshold of the room, only moving further in when my assistant exited, pulling the door shut gently behind her.

"I told you never to come here. Yet here you are." I frowned, concerned by her decision to come to my place of work. I ground out my cigarette.

"I told you I didn't want to see you anymore." I waved dismissively at the air, as though I could push aside and

erase our history as easily as my hand had passed through the last trailing puff of smoke.

Running one hand through my greying hair, I mustered my sternest tone, eager for this exchange to be over.

"I never promised you anything, Rachel. You need to grow up. It's over."

She took another step towards me, then placed one hand on her stomach.

"Jason, I won't give it up."

Her voice was loud, but it trembled, betraying her fear. When I didn't respond, she added, "I saw my doctor yesterday. It's a boy."

"Which you'll raise alone if you really refuse to get rid of it," I snapped. My heart raced, and I felt a wave of fury race through my bones. This would never work. I turned back to the window.

"You knew I didn't want a family."

Because you don't know how to be a dad! *my inner voice screamed. I shuddered as memories of my own childhood flashed to the surface. Unpleasant memories. I frowned, then forced myself to stand straighter.*

"Don't even think about blackmailing me, Rachel. I'm not an enemy you want to have. Not now, not ever."

Even with my back turned, I could feel her flinch. The air in the room had turned cold, as though her pain and sadness were sucking up all the heat.

"I would... I would never. I just thought, now that you've had time to think about it, you'd want to consider our options."

I spun around, then stepped purposefully over to stand directly in front of her.

Leaning close until my lips almost brushed her ear, I whispered, "I've already forgotten you, Rachel. Now you should forget me. I'm not about to let your carelessness ruin my life."

Now for the knockout punch. "You're not as special as you think you are."

I took a step back. Her face had gone slack, her eyes two round pools of disbelief. I turned my back to her, satisfied she'd gotten the message.

I awoke with a start, my entire body jerking so violently that I fell off the couch.

I'd dreamed. A horrible, confusing dream.

Then I heard the sound of paper sliding over carpet. I turned and saw an envelope lying on the floor by the door. Caden dropping off his sister's ID, I realized.

Forgetting the interruption, my thoughts returned to this latest mystery. Why would Adam dream such a thing?

Could it be a memory? From what I understood, Adam had lived life as a good person. He wasn't cruel.

More importantly, why would I experience any dreams or flashbacks at all with Adam gone? While I'd heard of shared dreams and memories with Hosts before, I'd never experienced any until today.

Yet it had felt so real. More like a memory than a fabrication.

Part of me knew that this should be impossible since the man in the dream hadn't looked or felt like Adam at all. For one thing, he was too old. It couldn't be part of Adam's past. Even more unsettling, I felt like I knew him, this Jason.

Like I'd seen him before.

No. This had to be another strange side effect of ejecting Adam from his body. A final ripple at the edge of the pond before he left, some sort of weird dream shadow or memory that he'd left behind.

I shakily sat up, then got up off the floor and returned to the couch. I stared out the suite window, replaying the strange dream again, wondering where it had come from and what significance it could have held for Adam. *Or for me.*

Surprisingly, I fell asleep again. I assume this was due to a new lack of control over my own exhaustion. I was discovering the downsides of choosing to oust Adam so I could travel alone in this body.

Jason surfaced again — as if Adam was taunting me with this unsolvable puzzle.

Time had moved backward. Jason pretended to be happy with this life he'd made, but inside he was very lonely. Driven by anger and a desire to overcome his history, Jason had amassed significant wealth and success in his chosen business. Still, sometimes the path he'd chosen, his methods, were not as honorable as his childhood self would have liked. He'd stepped on a few lives over the years, climbed over others to get where he wanted. He'd forgotten the call of compassion and integrity.

Ever so often, the regret and guilt became overwhelming — he hadn't started life with this warped soul but rather spun it anew out of all of the pains of the past.

At least he'd never had any children, never screwed up anyone else's future. A generous decision, or that's what he told himself when the loneliness poked his belly, when the urge to be something different dared to roll around his skull.

Then came the day when he met Rachel, and everything changed.

It was like he recognized her. She was that familiar song you can't name, but know lies within you, just on the edge of memory. The more time he spent with her, those needling moral regrets became longings. The call to be more like his child-self resurfaced; she made him think he could be good again. Empathy was still in his future — because she would accept nothing less.

The dawning sunlight crossed my face, stirring me from this latest dream. A few more hours had passed since I last awoke, and as I arose from my second dream, Evangeline also emerged from the bedroom, in sisterhood with the morning light.

She strolled over to the suite kitchenette, then spotted me frozen on the sofa.

"What are you pondering now?" she asked softly as she strolled over to pick up the envelope before the door.

I mustered a return smile. It felt twisted on my face, however. Lopsided.

"Just figuring out our game plan. I think you were right, last night. We need to catch a plane. Get out of here, disappear."

Weird. My voice sounded just a little off, a little deeper and richer than Adam's usual tone.

Evangeline had been examining the contents of the envelope, but she now looked up to stare at me. She'd noticed the difference too.

"Are you coming down with something?" IDs forgotten, she dropped the envelope on the kitchenette counter and walked over to the couch, her brow furrowing as she examined my face.

I realized I hadn't looked in a mirror since Adam left.

I jumped up, pushing past her as I began to walk quickly to the bathroom.

"No, just tired, I guess."

I slipped inside, closing the door behind me. Flipping on the light, I turned to the mirror.

Everything looked the same.

I leaned in closer until my nose almost touched the glass. Wait a minute. Were my eyes different? What color were Adam's eyes; weren't they blue? They seemed grayer now, darker. Or was it just my imagination?

A knock rang out on the door, causing me to jump. I smacked my head on the overhead light.

"Adam? Are you alright?"

I turned on the tap, quickly splashing some cold water on my face. "Fine, be out in a minute." I looked at Adam's reflection again.

Perhaps taking exclusive Possession had triggered some sort of chemical imbalance. Activated a little paranoia.

Swinging the door open, I stepped back outside and slipped past Evangeline, keeping my eyes averted. "We should get going. I saw a laundry bag in the bedroom closet. Let's throw in the rest of the clothes we bought, and get to the airport. We can get a carry-on bag there."

She nodded, heading toward the bedroom. When she reached the entranceway, she paused with her hand on the door handle, then turned back towards me.

"We're going to be ok, you know." She pursed her lips in a tight smile.

There she went again, trying to be strong, to reassure me! I realized that I did feel a bit better at her hollow optimism, even though logically, I knew that the odds were that we would not be ok.

Still, I wanted to believe that I'd made the right decision, staying here. I grabbed the IDs off the counter and shoved them into my pocket.

"Of course, we will. But we'd better get a move on."

She nodded, turning once more to leave the room. Before she could, I stopped her.

"Hey, Evangeline?"

She turned back, her smile softer than before. "Yes?"

I took a deep breath. "I know it's been crazy, but I'm glad I met you. I really am."

Her entire face blossomed with delight. "I feel the same way," she whispered, then turned into the bedroom, leaving me to enjoy the strange swell of my newly acquired heart alone.

FIVE
DIVINE INTERVENTION

As Evangeline and I settled into our seats, I cast a careful look about the plane. I couldn't shake an unsettled feeling I'd had since we left the hotel, couldn't lay down the hairs on the back of my neck. As I've mentioned before, I've learned to trust man's animal instincts, and at the moment, even with Adam gone, his body's animal radar was registering off the chart.

Given Adam's recent departure, I admit I wasn't entirely sure if my current anxiety was actually the result of his remains' makeup or my own. Either way, I was growing increasingly anxious with each passing minute, and I couldn't shake the feeling that we were being watched. Stalked.

"Everything all right?" Evangeline reached out to grasp my hand reassuringly.

"You don't look so good. I wouldn't have pegged you as a nervous flyer."

Not wanting to explain my true feelings, I nodded.

"A little nervous, but I'll be alright." I squeezed her hand in return, then placed it back on her lap.

Turning to look back up and down the aisle of the plane, I continued to search for anyone suspicious.

All the other passengers appeared occupied. A few were still putting away their carry-on's, while the rest were reading or speaking with one another, some already typing away on their laptops. No one was looking our way.

Still, I couldn't shake the feeling of looming doom.

I turned back towards Evangeline. She'd turned her head away and was looking out the passenger window. With her features relaxed, she looked about twelve. My desire to protect her was stronger than ever.

Silly human nerves. We would manage to disappear. The mafia men had lost our tail, at least for now, and with Adam dead, the Controller would have lost track of us as well. We were going to make it.

But I didn't really believe that. I can't say *why* I didn't believe it, but I didn't. I realized that day that I was much better at lying to others than to myself.

The jet started to taxi up the runway, and the flight attendant began her safety demonstration. I closed my eyes and took several deep breaths, determined to regain control.

As the plane soared off the runway and began its ascent, I started to think about our next steps.

Once we landed in New Orleans, the first thing we'd need to do was purchase new identities, I reasoned. While killing Adam would have made me untraceable to the Controller and her god Police, there was still the threat of Constantine's mafia counterparts, who may not have stopped looking for Evangeline. I needed to secure her safety and anonymity.

We'd need access to more cash soon, too. A bigger problem to solve, but not insurmountable given my abilities.

As the minutes passed uneventfully, my stolen heart slowed, and I began to relax. My body felt exhausted, and regardless of Host Adam's departure, it apparently still needed more rest.

Somewhere an hour into the flight, I fell asleep.

*   *   *

Agent Supervisor #1010 Report Addition:
Updated background information.

At the time my Agents submitted their initial reports on the failed Recall Attempts of god #201, his Host remained untraceable for unknown reasons.

As indicated previously, it was later discovered that #201 had evicted the primary soul of Host Adam the day prior. During the subsequent trial of #201, it was noted that a new rule should be created for gods Playground to cover this unexpected occurrence as well as to address the delay in the sharing of this vital information amongst our team.

While obviously not desirable, it is clear that Host eviction has never been strictly forbidden. It wasn't believed to be possible without the death of the Host body.

We deeply regret the additional challenges and disruption this oversight and lack of information flow created in the days that followed.

Investigative Report by god Policemen #806 & #807
re Attempted Recall of god #201 - Plane Incident
– Officer #806 Action Notes

By the time the Controller locked in our positions and initiated our transfer to the plane, #201 had allowed his Host to fall asleep in the passenger cabin of the aircraft.

My partner and I were new to the case but had been brought up to speed on #201's refusal to release his Host and return home at the end of his Vacation Period earlier that morning. It was deemed prudent to assume that all Hosts he now made contact with may be contaminated, or at the very least, were at risk of becoming aware of their role in gods Playground. It was unclear as to #201's state of mind and willingness to keep gods Playground a secret given his multiple Rule breaches and lack of communication with the Controller.

As planned, the Controller focused my entry on one of the Hosts in the plane's cockpit. As backup, the Controller placed my partner #807 in a male Host a few rows behind where #201 slept.

I was to induce the descent and eventual destruction of the craft, causing the subsequent termination of all contaminated Hosts on board, including #201's.

Prior to my arrival, the Pilot and Co-Pilot had been joking and making small talk as they monitored the automated flight control meters. The younger, junior Co-Pilot was complaining to the older, Senior Captain about his girlfriend troubles, and was waxing on the challenges of long-distance relationships. He then realized that the Captain had stopped responding to him.

The Co-Pilot turned to look at his superior. The Captain had slumped forward in his seat as I took Possession.

Reaching out to pull the Captain upright, the Co-Pilot asked with concern, "Sir, are you alright?"

I snapped the Pilot's eyes back open and straightened his spine stiffly as I took control. I shook off the other man's support.

"Fine, son, just fine." Turning to the junior Co-pilot, I forced the Captain's features into a sympathetic pucker.

"Guess I scared you there for a minute, eh? But I'm fine now."

Reaching out to turn off the autopilot and switch the controls to manual, I then grasped the yoke with one hand.

"Sir?" The younger Co-pilot studied me with growing concern, his own brow furrowing, but was apparently reluctant to question his superior.

I kept focused on my assigned task. Without looking at the Co-pilot, I/Captain said softly, "I'm sorry, buddy, but your day is about to get a whole lot worse than worrying about long-distance love, I'm afraid."

I then thrust the yoke forward, causing the plane to dive.

(Resumption of #201 narrative)

* * *

I dreamt. Once again, I was in Possession of the man I don't remember. The one called Jason.

He was with the same woman. This time, though, they weren't arguing. It appeared to be some time prior to the office confrontation.

They were in a kitchen, apparently making dinner together. She was much happier in this dream. Playful. She glowed with life and contentment as she danced about the lavish apartment, smiling and laughing.

"What are you cooking up? Hope you have greater success than last time," she teased. I/Jason waved her off, stirring something, but I could feel his shared joy, his depth of pleasure and satisfaction in her company.

"More wine, Rachel?" we asked.

She shook her head. "I think I'm high enough." She cast us a broad smile, then she and her long shining hair flowed across the room to slide gracefully onto the piano bench that stood before the baby grand by the window.

"Shall I play while you cook?"

Putting down the spoon, I walked across the room to join her. Sliding my arms across her shoulders, I leaned in close and whispered, "I have a better idea."

I awoke to the feeling of being roughly shaken. I wasn't sure how much time had passed, and in contrast to past Possession awakenings, I felt groggier as I surfaced out of this sleep. Perhaps that was to be expected, given my Host was gone and I was flying solo, no pun intended. Apparently, I was to become a regular dreamer too. At least this one had been more pleasant.

Evangeline was leaning over me, shaking my shoulders wildly.

"Adam. Adam, wake up! Something's wrong!" She sounded scared. I forgot about the dream.

I realized the plane's entire cabin was filled with panicked voices. Some passengers were whispering, some yelling, some sobbing. Then the aircraft lurched roughly, and most of the passengers emitted terrified screams.

I sat quickly upright, and my center of gravity pitched along with the plane's own wild roll, triggering the sensation of falling. As I braced myself against the forward seat, my gaze fell upon one of the stewardesses who was standing a few rows up the aisle behind a beverage cart. Her one hand was clinging on to the cart, either for support or in an effort to keep it from rolling down the aisle. With her free hand, she was grasping the arm of a tall businessman who was attempting to climb over the cart.

"Sir! Please return to your seat! The seatbelt light is on. You need to sit down! I'm sure the Captain will get us through this turbulence soon. I need to put this cart away. Sir!"

Turbulence? This was no turbulence, at least not like any I'd experienced before.

It felt like the plane was being jerked downward and upward every few moments, like a gyrating, angry snake squirming under a predator's grip. It felt more like a wrestling match, more like….

Oh no! It couldn't be. They wouldn't!

I wrested myself from Evangeline's grasp and released my seat belt. As I rose to my feet, she reached out and snagged the tail of my jacket.

"Adam! What are you doing? I think we should stay in our seats!"

I carefully peeled her fingers from the hem of my jacket.

"I'm going to try to help."

Without waiting to see if she accepted my explanation, I began to make my way down the aisle towards the cockpit, pausing to grip the back of each seat for balance as I passed.

Then the plane lurched upward again, and I was thrown roughly against the seat to my left, momentarily knocking the wind out of me. The cabin filled with more terrified screams, and I was reminded of the reliability of man's overwhelming and consistent fear of death.

While many of you claim a belief in the Ever After, you nevertheless do not take kindly to the idea of your own demise. You prefer to cling to this Earthbound life. Most of you hold tight to this existence until the last strangled breath.

The air of the plane was now heavy with that fear, with your high-pitched sounds and the sour, electric smell of terror. Rightly so, I figured, as so far, it looked like this was not going to end well.

Someone was trying to crash this plane. I was certain of it.

I succeeded in regaining my balance and stepped forward until I was standing behind the man on the beverage cart. He'd managed to get one hand and one knee on top and was attempting to pull up his other leg, all while swiping his second hand wildly at the defending stewardess. While his progress was slow, he was successful in toppling half empty pop cans and water jugs amid his struggle with the stewardess.

Without a word, I grasped the back of his collar with one hand and the back of his pant belt with the other. Then I pulled with everything I had, lifting him off the cart. I tossed him into an empty plane seat to my left.

Turning back, I surmised the cart climber was correct, and there really was no quick way around the obstruction. Not without backing the cart up to the galley of the plane, a maneuver that would take much too long, particularly with all the distraught passengers, some of whom were out of their seats. If I wanted to get to the cockpit, I'd need to find another way.

I looked into the eyes of the stewardess clinging to the other side of the cart. They were widened ovals of stress and fright. She didn't look like she'd be open to suggestions. That was alright since I wasn't in the mood to negotiate.

"Hey, sweetie," I whispered softly, ending with a smile. I locked my gaze warmly with hers.

Then I Jumped.

I felt immediately lighter and realized my new temporary Host was feeling a bit faint. After expertly suppressing her essence into merciful slumber, I shook her head and brought her senses back online, her long blond locks flying about our face as I looked back at my deserted Adam body.

My primary home lay slumped across the top of the beverage cart. It looked unconscious, but so far, my body was still breathing. At least for now.

I couldn't allow myself to worry about my favored home, however. Ignoring the urge to peel his eyes open and Jump back into Adam's body, I made my new female Host spin around, abandoning him where he lay. New stewardess me started running towards the front of the plane. Other than my momentary adventure in the businessman's tart, I'd never Possessed a woman before. I couldn't help but notice the warmer, peaceful feeling of the body, the total lack of burning aggression even in this unusual circumstance.

Shaking off this unfamiliar experience, I dashed towards the cockpit door. I could see that a second female stewardess was pounding on the cabin door with one hand while hopelessly shaking the locked door handle with the other.

"Sir, Captain, what's going on in there?"

As I reached her side, I could hear thumps coming from within the locked cockpit, along with muffled shouts and grunts. I surmised that the Captain and Co-pilot were engaged in a struggle, which meant one was still in possession of himself. It also explained the up and down flight pattern.

"Can you open the door?" I gasped, my stewardess Host's voice high and feminine with unmasked alarm.

The second stewardess turned to me, her own eyes glazed and moist.

"You know I can't! Anti-terrorist measures during flight; they've locked it! But something's wrong! They sound like they're fighting in there. Do you think the Pilot's lost it? Or maybe it's the Co-Pilot. What should we do? Oh my god!"

Not God. Controller. Only she could stop this now.

My hunch had to be correct. The god Police must be behind this insanity. They were attempting to crash the plane in order to kill Adam, to trigger an end to my Possession and send me home.

None of this made sense. I can honestly say I was surprised.

Despite what Earthbounds may judge as our god disregard for humanity, the rules around Possession have always been clear. While we may interfere with your "daily lives" when we take Possession of an individual Host, we were never to influence a group of Earthbounds in any global way.

During the act of Possession, visiting gods must act within the realm of possibility of their Host.

They cannot speak of, nor demonstrate, their unique powers in any way discernable to other surrounding Earthbounds.

Earthbounds cannot become aware of the act of Possession.

Gods cannot act in such a way as to create a global influence, nor change the expected path of their current Host in any meaningful way.

Yet as the plane continued to hurtle towards its likely demise, the only conclusion I could come to was that the god Police didn't care if they killed everyone else on board in the process of reclaiming me.

They must fear that I might alert humanity to the act of Possession. If so, then I was indeed a doomed god; they saw me as a renegade, a turncoat. Even so, I never thought the Controller would allow the god Police to just kill you off at random. Their actions on this plane, their disregard for their impact on the surrounding Hosts; it went against every rule of the Playground as I'd understood it. My world as I knew it was a lie.

But how had they found me? My mind raced, frantic to solve this more urgent puzzle. *How were they still tracking Adam's body, with the Host soul gone? I'd been so confident killing him would work.*

"Hello, 201."

My ponderings were interrupted by a sickly smooth male voice that spoke behind me, and I quickly spun my gal around to face whoever had called me by my real name.

I'd barely completed my turn when the tall, fair-haired young man who'd uttered my god number looked me in the eye, then placed his hands on my current Host's elegant thin neck.

He began to squeeze. As his strong hands tightened on the stewardess's thin frame, I quickly realized we were no physical match for our attacker.

Lacing her fine fingers around our assailant's thick hands, I struggled to keep her conscious as I rolled her eyes desperately down the aisle.

Then I managed to lock gazes with another young man wearing a University of Chicago sweatshirt. He was jumping up from a seat several rows back, just ahead of the beverage cart. Likely he intended to come to the strangled stewardess's rescue. Gotcha!

I Jumped again, leaving my poor stewardess at the attacker's mercy.

Including her assailant and the other suspect in the cockpit that meant there were at least two god Policemen on board. Hopefully, that was all of them. They did like to travel in pairs.

But how to get into the cockpit? We were screwed! Still, I wasn't about to give up.

I was becoming quicker at this Suppression thing and managed to lurch Chicago U boy quickly upright and back into a standing position. Turning to glance at my original attacker, I could see he'd already tossed the stewardess aside. She lay gasping on the floor, likely wondering where the last few minutes went and why she couldn't breathe.

He ignored her struggles and instead cast a searching look up the aisle. He knew I'd Jumped! He was looking for me. Rats! I should have kept Chicago U seated until I could come up with a plan.

Too late, he'd spotted me. The god Policeman made his Host dash down the aisle, and he was upon me in seconds.

I swung Chicago U's arm, clocking my pursuer across the lower jaw. He staggered backward, falling into the lap of the elderly woman in the opposite aisle seat.

Before he could disentangle himself from the screaming woman (who'd begun beating him with her laptop), I quickly began to run forward, intending to go back to the cockpit door.

I'd barely advanced two rows before I felt a sudden weight on my back. I fell with a thud to the aisle floor. Someone had jumped me from behind, knocking the wind out of my Host, Chicago U.

"Cease immediately, 201!"

An elderly man's voice? The Policeman had switched Hosts. Then the god Police could Body Jump also! So much for my one advantage.

Before I could ponder this new challenge, he'd placed his knee on the back of our neck. Was choking me to death really his only move?

Despite his youth, my current Host proved no match for the elderly Host's quick assault, and our consciousness began to fade from lack of oxygen. I rolled our eyes upward in hopes of seeing anyone. Anyone?

As luck would have it, just two rows up, an attractive, middle-aged woman was leaning out of her seat, screaming at my attacker.

"Stop! Let him go, you monster!"

I locked eyes with my hero gratefully and Jumped again.

She was stronger and more present than the previous Hosts and took a minute to Suppress. Panicked by the delay, I rushed to make her rise. Then I felt a hand on my arm.

"Cathy, what are you doing?"

I looked down at the man sitting in the window seat. His face was pale, his mouth agape with each panted breath. Her husband?

"Someone's gotta kick some ass here, sweetheart, or we're all gonna die."

Ok, I admit that was a little too macho for an elderly housewife, but I had no time for editorial planning.

Brushing his hand off, I made hot grandma rush up the aisle and once again managed to reach the cockpit.

Then I made the mistake of glancing back.

The god Policeman in Possession of the elderly man caught my lady's eyes and realized I'd pulled a switch. He leapt up, abandoning the gasping Chicago U boy where he lay.

The Policeman glanced about, then reached his gnarled hands into the seat just one row ahead. Grasping the shirt of a broad businessman in a grey suit who was cowering there, he pulled the younger man's face close to his elder Host's own.

The elderly Host crumbled to the floor, and the businessman got out of his seat, frightened no more.

As my new younger pursuer started to make his way back up the aisle, Chicago U came back into consciousness and lurched to his own feet. Giving a curdling football yell, he launched himself onto the back of the first person he saw. It was the god Policeman's new Host, the young businessman.

Thanks, bud!

Not waiting to watch their struggle, I turned back to the cockpit, my mind racing with what to do next.

Then the cockpit door opened and a man burst out, knocking the second stewardess backward. *Hallelujah!*

Obviously stunned, his face bloody, the Co-Pilot leaned against the now-open door.

"Help! I need help! The Pilot's trying to crash the plane! I can't stop him!"

Before anyone else could react, I made my cute grandma charge forward and leap onto the Co-pilot's chest, causing us both to tumble backward into the cockpit.

Kicking the door shut with one high-heeled boot, I then climbed off the Co-Pilot and quickly re-locked the cockpit door.

Glancing at the Pilot's chair, I could see it was still occupied by a wiry, built man of about fifty. He sat hunched over the yoke, brow twisted and jaw locked, arms thrust forward as he pushed the plane into a deeper dive. Consumed with his task, he appeared content to ignore our commotion behind him. The Co-Pilot, meanwhile, lay gasping on the floor where we'd pushed him, evidently stunned. I didn't think grandma/I could tackle the Captain alone, however.

Reaching out to grasp the face of the Co-Pilot with grandma's soft hands, I locked eyes with him.

"Ok, pal, snap out of it, you can do this."

The Jump was instantaneous. He was already exhausted, overwhelmed, and apparently in shock. He gave up without a fight.

As grandma stumbled backward into the cockpit door, slowly coming back to herself, I made my Co-Pilot rise to his feet.

I placed one arm around the neck of the Captain, putting him in a headlock. I then yanked the Pilot backward, intending to pull him out of his seat.

Acknowledging my presence for the first time since we'd entered, he began to struggle and claw at my arm with one hand, although he kept the other hand determinedly pressed against the downward yoke. Such dedication!

Nevertheless, moments later, my new younger Host was able to pin the Pilot half in, half out of his chair. We had him subdued, at least for the moment, although I wasn't sure how long that would hold true.

I reached out with my other hand to pull the yoke back towards me, attempting to right the plane and pull it out of its dive.

Now what? I wasn't sure what to do next. Warning buzzers were still ringing throughout the cockpit, and I didn't really know how to read the controls. An urgent voice was blaring out of the speaker — one of the Air Traffic Controllers demanding to know the status of our flight. It no longer felt like we were falling (the plane did feel more level), but I couldn't be certain. Were we safe?

The Captain and I were twisted together in an awkward embrace across the Pilot's chair. My body was braced over his lap, and I was wrapped uncomfortably sideways, with one arm still encircling his neck in a vice grip, while with the other, I continued to pull backward on the yoke. He seemed successfully trapped between my body and the arm of the chair, but he wasn't passing out, and I needed to focus on flying the plane.

He twisted his head to the side, then gasped, "201! Cease and desist."

I squeezed harder, cutting off the rest of his words. His eyes bulged. I leaned closer until our cheeks touched, so I could whisper in his ear.

"Sorry, not feeling like following the rules today. Guess I'm just not ready to go home yet, asshole."

Then I heard movement behind me. I'd forgotten about Grandma!

I turned my head to see what she was up to. The god Policeman saw his opportunity and took advantage of my distraction and weakening grip.

He reached up with his left hand. With the arm that wasn't fully pinned, the one that had been flailing by his side.

Then he pushed a button on the panel above us. A big nasty looking red button. He immediately stabbed at a second button beside it. As I futilely yanked his arm back too late, I read the labels on the buttons. The red one was called "Arm." Its neighbor was named "Activate."

"What have you done?"

I had a reflexive urge to call up for a pilot Memory Upload, then remembered that the Controller wasn't about to answer my call for helpful information.

I once again loosened my grip on the Pilot so I could lean closer to the raised panel. Until I could see the smaller letters imprinted above the pair of red buttons.

The Policeman sneered from within the Pilot's chiseled face, then took a massive gulp of air.

"It says Jettison," he gasped.

When I didn't immediately respond, he took another deep inhalation, then hissed, "Oh wait, perhaps without the Controller's help, you need the layman's term? I've initiated a fuel dump."

Having now fully regained his breath, he mustered a self-satisfied chuckle.

"Standard protocol in an emergency crash landing. You'll have no fuel in minutes. Game over, 201. Checkmate."

He looked like he was about to say more, but he never got the chance. Instead, his head rocked sideways as he was snapped out of my headlock and tumbled to the floor.

Grandma had clocked him with the fire extinguisher.

I turned to look at her, surprised but relieved.

She offered me a brave smile. "You looked like you could use some help with that nut." Then she frowned. "I think I blacked out there for a minute or two. I remember getting up to help that nice boy, but now I find myself in the cockpit."

Shrugging, she placed her hand gently on my shoulder. "Can you land this plane alone, young man? What can I do to help?"

Once again, I marveled at the mystery of the human spirit. Either it unraveled with panic at the first opportunity, or instead, chose to fight and persevere against all odds. I smiled genuinely for the first time since boarding this flight. So often, it is the sweetest looking ones that come out of left field, that somehow have it in them to rise to the occasion.

Nodding, I smiled widely with gratitude, hoping I could convince her that I knew what I was doing. Pushing the unconscious Pilot Host further into the corner to clear some leg room, I slipped into the Captain's seat.

"Yes. Without enough fuel, I'll need to conduct an emergency landing."

My mind raced. I'd never been in Possession of a pilot before. What did I know about planes? *Got it!*

"We need to radio for help. To ask them where to land. Here." I gestured to the Co-Pilot seat. "Sit there. Put on the headset and respond to the Air Traffic Control. Tell them we're almost out of fuel."

I continued to study the controls, calling up every past Host memory in rapid succession, vainly searching for anything that would help me fly this plane.

Grandma nodded back and sat down before silently slipping the headset onto her head. She then leaned forward and looked at the controls. She surprised me by quickly flipping a toggle switch, causing static to come over the speaker. Smart gal!

Placing her hand to the mouthpiece, she said firmly, "Hello? Can anyone hear me? I'm a passenger on flight 702 from Chicago. We need help. We have almost no fuel, and we've lost our pilot. The Co-Pilot needs help to land this plane ASAP. Hello?"

* * *

Investigative Report by god Policeman #807
re Attempted Plane Crash Incident - Officer Action Notes

After repeated Body Jumps between myself and #201, he managed to lock himself in the cockpit with my partner, the Co-Pilot, and the old woman. I called up to the Controller, requesting my recall.

I'd hoped she could place me in a new Host inside the cockpit, either the old woman or the Co-Pilot, whichever Host was not currently Possessed by #201. I couldn't reach either of these Hosts myself via Jumping due to the door between us, so this seemed the most reasonable next plan of action.

When the Controller didn't immediately respond, I was forced to make an alternative action decision. I decided to employ another Jump in order to take Possession of a new Host outside the cockpit — one with more influence on #201's interests.

I approached Host Adam's unconscious body, which was still draped across the beverage cart. I opened his eyes and went in, leaving my previous Host.

I made Host Adam rise, and while at the time unaware of the original Host's eviction, I found the hollow body was much more difficult to maneuver than typical. Apparently, without the original Host spirit, it was much heavier. This officer would like to record to the investigative summary that after inadvertently experiencing this atypical Possession, it is my opinion that Possession of the dead is not advised for Policeman, except perhaps as a last resort.

After some effort, I managed to walk the Adam body back to the seat where the female Host Evangeline was still seated.

"Adam? Are you alright? What just happened?" The plane rolled again. I assumed my partner was struggling with #201 and his current Host inside the cockpit.

Host Evangeline screamed, "Oh my god, there goes the plane again!" and then she grabbed onto my arm.

She appeared confused. She'd seen us draped unconscious over the cart, yet now we'd arisen again. Hosts are naturally suspicious of abrupt changes in another Host's consciousness, plus the plane was still pitching about. She was afraid.

My plan was to take her to the cockpit and force her to convince #201 to open the door. I thought he would respond to her pleas. Our records showed that he was obsessed with her and had become overly attached to her Earthbound affairs.

I began to drag her out of the seat. I instructed her, "Come with me; we have to help. You need to talk to 201, help me make him open the door."

She resisted. She started screaming,

"Who's Towen?" (Interesting. I realized she'd misheard my reference to #201 and assumed it was a name). "What's going on, Adam?" she asked me again.

I realized I'd made an error in referring to #201 by name. I was now Adam, yet I wasn't acting as she expected and had confused her further. The lurching of the plane was also causing her extreme distress. Her mood had become non-negotiable.

I revised my plan again and proceeded to lift her up on Host Adam's shoulders. I then carried her as I walked up the aisle. I hoped once we reached the cockpit, I could cause her to scream loud enough for #201 to hear her and cause him to open the door, to rush to her defense.

To get around the beverage cart, I stepped onto the man's lap in the seat left of the cart. I tossed Host Evangeline into the next row, the one ahead of the cart. I then climbed over the chair and, unfortunately, had to subdue several passengers in the row ahead in order to reclaim woman Evangeline from them. I then carried her as planned to the cockpit door.

She struggled against me, predictably frightened by my actions. I placed her on the floor beside the cockpit door, admittedly unsure how to regain her trust. I told her that the plane was about to crash and that she and I needed to convince the Pilot to open the cockpit door. I lied and told her I would land the plane if I got inside.

She didn't believe me. "You're not a pilot. None of this makes sense!" She was terrified and still suspicious of me. "Adam, you're acting crazy. Why were you so rough? Do you think this the mob's doing? Their men don't do suicide missions; why'd they try to crash the plane? We should strap back into our seats! We need to...."

In a last attempt, I squeezed her arm hard, but she wouldn't make a sound nor call out. She just stared at me with her big eyes that kept getting bigger. She was useless.

I needed a new action plan. I pushed her aside and began to search the galley. I soon discovered a purse belonging to a stewardess, inside which I found a nail file. I began to attempt to pick the cockpit door lock.

At the same time, I called up to the Controller again in hopes of yet obtaining an assisted transfer to the woman in the cockpit. My partner needed my help, but the Controller still did not respond to my page.

I do not understand why the Controller was offline. However, I take full responsibility for my actions.

(Resumption of #201 narrative)

* * *

174

After a brief conversation with the Air Traffic Controller, he confirmed that while we were horribly off course and flying at too low an altitude, he had managed to redirect any surrounding flights. So, at least the immediate danger of a mid-air collision was no longer an issue. We began to discuss options for an emergency landing.

Given our fuel dump, he admitted that we'd be lucky if we could sustain flight for more than another fifteen to twenty minutes. Despite this glaring fact, I spent the next few minutes arguing with him about where we could land. He wanted to redirect me back to Chicago O'Hare, which was insane. And you wonder why we consider human Hosts irrational!

Grandma had helpfully interjected that we'd never make it to O'Hare, as we'd already been in the air for well over an hour. She had remained impressively calm throughout the exchange, although her voice had risen as our mutual exasperation with the Air Traffic Controller grew.

He then proposed several abandoned airstrips south of the city, but these too were located too far for us to reach before we'd be running on nothing more than fumes.

I realized that I could hear the sound of someone jiggling the cockpit door lock. Not someone I'd like to let in, I wagered. And what of Evangeline? I worried about how she was faring with Adam slumped over the beverage cart.

"Wait, I have it!" cute grandma said, grasping my arm and pulling my concentration away from thoughts of my love and the mystery foe beyond the door.

Focus on landing this plane!

"I'm open to suggestions since the advice we've been getting is weak at best," I said with a smile.

"The river! We can land in the Mississippi!" Her features relaxed, and she smiled openly back at me, certain she'd saved us all. Certain that I'd now save us all.

Not only had I never flown a plane before, but now to attempt a narrow river landing? Even with the questionable help of the Air Traffic Controller, I doubted I could pull it off.

Yet she was right. We really had run out of options.

Nodding, I flipped on my cabin mike and began to inform the passengers of the impending crash-landing.

* * *

Investigative Report by god Policeman #807
re Attempted Plane Crash Incident - Officer Exit Notes

The voice of the Co-Pilot Host came over the plane intercom. I was certain that #201 was in Possession of this Host, as he tried to prepare the passengers for an attempted landing of the craft in a nearby river.

I realized that given the Controller's unresponsiveness and my partner's apparent incapacitation, that there is was nothing more for me to do at this time. There appeared no way to recover #201 in this current scenario. Additionally, we'd created way too much disruption; Earthbounds would investigate, and there was the possibility of survivors being interviewed. Time to regroup.

So I released Host Adam and returned home to record my Officer Notes and await further instruction. It would be reasonable to assume that should #201's Host survive the crash and remain on gods Playground, that #201 would likely choose to return to his favored Host. Either way, a second attempt to reclaim the fugitive would be made within the next few hours, once human attention around his Host had dissipated.

(Resumption of #201 narrative)

* * *

After another wasted moment spent arguing with Air Traffic Control about our plan to execute a controlled ditch of the aircraft in the Mississippi, he finally realized that I wasn't in the mood to negotiate and began to actually help us.

I pleaded confusion due to hitting my head, and he reminded me of the operation of the craft controls. Together we redirected the plane over the Mississippi's path. Within minutes of initiating a fairly controlled descent, I spotted the winding river below.

As we descended further and approached the water's surface, the plane suddenly fell eerily silent.

Turning to look at Grandma, I could see her face had turned white.

"The engines stopped," she whispered.

We'd run out of fuel while still a few hundred feet above the ground and were now gliding on nothing but our own momentum and the craft's wings.

Turning to look out the front window, I focused intently on the plane's nose while also watching the Artificial Horizon Indicator display for our levelness to the surface below. The air around me felt thick and pressing, as though pulsing with a heartbeat of its own.

I felt a rush of anger. Tough grandma didn't deserve this. The unconscious pilot beside me didn't deserve this. All those people behind me, all those souls, they didn't deserve this. This wasn't just happening to me, and it wasn't just about Evangeline anymore, either.

I realized I hadn't thought kindly about home, or about the Controller, for a while. Somewhere along the way, I'd changed. This Possession had changed me. Evangeline, and the actions of the god Police, and my flashbacks or Adam's memories or whatever they were, they'd all played a part. Gods Playground wasn't a Playground for me any longer.

My understanding of Hosts had transformed. Just the word Host felt wrong. Thin. I felt a connection to Earthbounds that I'd never experienced before, as well as a strange protective urge. No, that wasn't accurate either.

I felt driven, possessed. Ha! How the tables had turned. I needed to do this for them. I *wanted* to do this for them. Because in many ways, I now *was* one of them.

I was different, and I think I liked it.

I clicked on the passenger cabin intercom. "Brace for impact," I said softly, then placed it back in its holster.

As the plane's belly touched the water's surface, I was rocked back in my seat, striking the side of my head against the bulkhead. Everything went dark for a moment.

I reopened my eyes in time to watch as waves of displaced water rushed over the cockpit windows. The aircraft dipped, then rose and dropped again, before coasting gracefully to a stop mid-river, just as picture-perfect as a stone cast across a still pond.

I must have hit my head harder than I realized because the room spun again. I allowed my eyes to close and smiled, pleased the worst was over. Everyone was safe. Evangeline was safe.

Then I remembered who she trusted.

Adam!

Struggling Co-Pilot Host to his feet, I turned and unlocked the cabin door. Everything swirled again, and I was forced to brace myself against the door, causing it to smash into the wall. I paused, leaning on it before stumbling forward.

"Young man, are you alright? We need to get everyone off this plane before it sinks." Grandma's voice sounded milky, as though we were already underwater.

What I needed was to get back to Adam. I lurched through the doorway, intending to head down the aisle back to the beverage cart, where I hoped Adam still lay as I'd left him.

My eyes were doing weird things now, and I struggled to navigate the aisle as the world faded in and out of focus. Darkness crept further into my field of vision, a diminishing black halo that threatened to consume all the light.

Luckily, it turned out I didn't have very far to go.

My leading toe caught under something, and I crashed to the ground. I rolled over to see what had tripped me.

Adam lay on his back, crumpled on the floor like a discarded rag doll. Blood trickled from a small cut on his left temple. I glanced back up the aisle. The beverage cart was just where I expected it, a few rows back. How had he moved?

Then that halo shrunk again, and I felt my current Host's consciousness starting to slip away.

Grasping Adam's shirt, I pulled myself on top of him, then took his face in my hands. He was still warm. *Yes!*

I used both thumbs to peel his eyes open. I went in without any effort; it was as though he were waiting for me.

As I settled back into Adam, I felt the room spin. He was even groggier than my past Host, apparently. The irony of the moment struck me, but there was no going back now.

Then it dawned on me — while I was about to fall into unconsciousness, I had also, in these last moments on the plane, fully awoke.

My misconduct and rule-breaking behavior may have begun days ago, triggered by some strange impulse, by my infatuation with Evangeline. Ok, correction, my love for her; if that was what this truly was.

Either way, since then, my motives had evolved. They had taken on a new life. I was no longer a mere spectator; I was a part of humanity now.

As Adam's eyelids began to slide shut, I made a decision.

It wasn't about the wager anymore; it hadn't been for a while now. Nor was it about ascending to a higher plane.

I chose Evangeline.

I chose Earthbounds.

I would let my god self go. I would be this new me. I wasn't #201 anymore.

I was Adam.

SIX

A HOST IN SHEEP'S CLOTHING

Despite my grand thought before falling into unconsciousness that I'd truly become Adam, in my subsequent dreams, I was Jason again.

No, that's not quite right. This time, this dream, felt more like I was a spectator, observing Jason from the outside. I felt disconnected from him, yet at the same time, somehow, I still was Jason.

He was younger. Although tall, definitely not an adult yet, maybe nine at most. He was standing at a closed bedroom door, leaning his ear against it, listening intently.

The voices of two people shouting could be heard bouncing like ping pong balls up and down the hall, fading in and out with each angry word.

We flicked our fingers together subconsciously. Every few seconds, we shifted from one foot to the other, as if undecided whether to stay safe behind the door or to burst through to whatever lay waiting beyond. To intervene?

Then we heard the cry and the thump as she fell to the floor.

Jason slumped, and we turned back to the bed. Walking away from the door, a feeling of unrelenting misery washed over us as we crawled back under the covers.

Beep, beep, beep.

Coming out of the foggy-headedness of sleep, I couldn't at first identify the sharp, high pitched sound. My mind was still clouded by the dream of Jason. I tried to open my eyes, but they weren't cooperating.

I was beginning to think these dreams weren't Adam's. They weren't part of his past or his memories.

Somehow, they were mine.

They had to be part of a past Vacation. It was the only thing that made sense, that explained where these memories could have come from. A download mix-up, perhaps. But why the mixed timeline for the Jason Vacation and Adam's? Why couldn't I recall the Jason Vacation clearly, except during sleep?

Then there's the real kicker, the question I'd been avoiding.

Why didn't Jason feel like a Host?

Beep, beep, beep.

There it was again, as though insisting I wake up. I began to notice other distant sounds. Multiple voices speaking softly, a phone ringing.

I stirred and heard a soft rustle. This one I got right away. It was the sound of starched sheets sliding across one another.

Shaking off the last troublesome vestiges of my dream, I opened my eyes. Yup, I was in a hospital bed.

My body was coming around, but I still felt sluggish; it was difficult to move. Either Adam was more hurt than I'd realized, or he'd been drugged. I rolled my eyes to survey the room and saw a woman with long black hair sitting on the end of my bed. Her back was to me, and she was staring up at a television suspended from the opposite wall.

A newscast was playing, zoomed in on a journalist who was chatting excitedly into his microphone. He gestured at a scene behind him.

It was the plane, half-submerged in the river.

The woman before me ran her hand nervously through her long hair, and I heaved a sigh of relief as I recognized the gesture as Evangeline's. Why was her hair different? I struggled into a sitting position.

Hearing my movement, she spun around.

"Adam! About time you woke up. I was beginning to think you were only staying unconscious to avoid explaining yourself." She gave me a half-smile, then reached out to turn off the television.

"Wait!" I croaked, raising my hand.

Evangeline pursed her lips, then turned back to glance at the screen.

The newscast had cut to an image of the plane's Co-Pilot. He was surrounded by journalists and men in suits with stern expressions. His eyes darted back and forth as though searching for answers in the crowd, his face white with lingering strain.

"I'm sorry." He attempted to wave off the sea of microphones that hung about his face. "I really have nothing else to add at this point."

"I don't recall landing the plane in the river." His eyes still dancing nervously. "I, I'm sure with time, it will come back to me. I have nothing further to add except to say that I'm glad that no one was seriously hurt and that no lives were lost."

"What about the Captain? Why do you think he lost it?" pressed a reporter, holding his microphone closer.

"I don't know what happened to the Captain, why he did what he did. I can't explain it." The Co-Pilot seemed to recoil into himself, obviously spent.

A grey-haired man in a dark blazer now stepped forward from the group of suits standing behind the Co-Pilot and took up position in front of him, apparently an airline spokesman.

"That's it for now, no more questions," he said firmly. "You can all appreciate that our investigation is just beginning, and we will share our findings as we progress."

He turned back to pat the Co-Pilot on the shoulder. "Needless to say, Co-Pilot Wilson here is a hero, and we are all grateful for his courageous efforts today. We now need to get him to debrief so we can get him closer to some well-earned rest. He's said all he will say today."

Raising his palm high against the media's outburst of questions, he added, "The airline will issue further statements and updates as our investigation progresses, and as appropriate. Thank you, everyone."

I waved at Evangeline, and she switched it off.

She studied me for a moment. "I was on the news too," she said, apparently mistaking my obsession with the Co-Pilot's statement for worry about our possible exposure.

"It was shortly after the crash, once we'd all been ferried to the shore." She brushed her new hair off her face. "They'd gathered us all beside the waiting ambulances. Everyone was getting examined, checked for injuries, although no one that I saw seemed seriously hurt. It really is a miracle."

She sighed, fiddling with the blankets at the bottom of my bed. "I'd been arguing with the Ambulance attendant because I wanted to ride with you to the hospital. You were still unconscious, and I was really worried. His partner was examining that older woman, the one that was in the cockpit with the Co-Pilot. While we were arguing, a reporter came up, and that older woman, she started talking to him."

Evangeline's expression darkened with worry. "She went on and on about her role in it all, about what she believed had happened, about the struggle between the Pilot and Co-Pilot and how she'd helped. I tried to move away, but I saw myself captured on the film clip when the interview replayed earlier — when I was waiting for you to wake up."

Evangeline ran her hand through her hair again. "That's why I dyed my hair. Can you believe they sell hair dye in a hospital gift shop?"

She blushed, offering me her crooked smile. "How bad does it look?"

This was not good. I struggled to decide what to do next. I felt weird, off — as if my thoughts were drenched in thick muck.

Evangeline sat down on the bed and grasped my hand.

"Take it easy, Adam; you still look a little out of it. The doctors said they didn't find anything serious. It's likely just a mild concussion."

Sitting back, she released my hand to place both of hers on her hips. Her expression turned stern, although I could see her heart wasn't in it.

"Now, Adam Juri, tell me what was up with you on that plane! You got up thinking you could help, *how* I don't know, but then you collapsed onto the beverage cart. I wasn't sure what had happened to you."

Evangeline stood up and began to pace about the room, her thin arms fluttering at her sides.

"People were screaming and fighting; it was all so crazy for a while." Heaving a sigh, she turned her big eyes towards me, their corners narrowing as she studied me again.

"Then you woke up, you got off the beverage cart, and you grabbed me, carried me forward. You said you knew the Captain and needed my help to get him to open the cabin door. You called him Towen. It was all very weird." She frowned.

Towen?

Then it hit me. My god name.

2-0-1. The god Police must have said my name, must have spoken to her; clearly, they'd also taken Possession of Adam. I guess in all the confusion, she'd heard Towen. But what had the God Police made Adam do while I was in the cabin?

I had no way of knowing, no way to access the memories. Apparently, while I was busy in the cockpit, Adam hadn't been on his best behavior while interacting with Evangeline.

What now?

As I struggled to decide what to do next, Evangeline grasped my hands in both of her own once again.

"Did you really know the Captain? How did you realize he was trying to crash the plane? What was going on, Adam? Why were you so rough?" Her beautiful face was turned in with confusion, and I cringed, upset that the God Police had used Adam in my absence in this way.

While I could grudgingly admire their creativity in doing so, any fleeting feeling of respect was squelched by the flood of anger I now felt. Adam was mine, not theirs! I was Adam. Possession should no longer be an option for him. Not for us.

More worrisome, I still couldn't understand how they'd tracked us to the plane in the first place. I was certain that by ejecting the original Adam, his body would have become untraceable from that moment onward.

Something wasn't adding up.

"How did you know the pilot was trying to crash the plane?" Evangeline pressed again, unaware of my separate ponderings. Pursing her lips, she repeated softly, "You were so rough, so determined I could help. I still don't understand why."

Once again, I didn't answer, for I had not been there. I didn't know what Adam had done in my absence while possessed by the god Police.

Then I had another realization. I knew how they'd found me.

It was her.

When I didn't respond, Evangeline nodded her head vigorously. "Sorry, this is all too much for you right now, isn't it? Your head injury; you're confused. It's going to be alright." She glanced toward the hospital room doorway.

"While you were unconscious, I called Caden. He's on his way, flew out a few hours ago. He should be here any time now." She patted my arm. "I told him we lost our borrowed IDs in the crash. He can help us, I'm sure of it."

I did feel confused. Certainly out of control. Had several hours really passed since the crash? That Jason dream had shaken me more than I wanted to admit. If this lack of clarity was part of being human, it was a part of humanity I could do without.

"You called Caden?" I shook my head. I was having trouble breathing. They were tracing her, using her to find me. *Idiot!* I should have anticipated this outcome. This was bad.

"Listen. Caden can't help us. I care about you, Evangeline, but we need to separate. Now! You have to leave."

Evangeline shook her head. "I know, I know, the mob must have gotten our trail again somehow. And my image on the news doesn't help. I'm sure it won't be long before they find out where we are." She grasped my hand tightly. "But I'm not leaving without you, Adam. Are you well enough to travel?" She turned to look toward the doorway again.

I shook off her hand so I could grab her shoulders firmly in both of my hands, turning her face towards me to force eye contact.

"Evangeline, stop! Listen to me! There's no time. You need to get out of here, now! Just get as far from me as you can."

My head spun, and for a moment, I thought I'd pass out.

"They're tracking you," I said less forcefully. "It's the only thing that makes sense."

I had to make her understand. I couldn't let the god Police hurt her because of me.

"It's not the mob. The men on the plane, the whole crash… it's not about you anymore. It's about me."

I could see she didn't believe me, but still, I pressed.

"They're trying to kill Adam, to get to me. They know that you and I are together, that I'm helping you. They must have found me by tracing your movements."

She stood up, looking about the room. "What are you talking about? You're Adam. Who'd be after you? I don't understand." She rubbed her forehead.

"You're just confused because of hitting your head. You were out for hours. I'm sure it messed you up, the concussion." Her pitch rising, she threw another glance at the doorway, then gave me a pleading look.

"The mob, they want **me** dead, because of Constantine. No one is after you." She was staring at me, desperate for me to believe her version, for us to reconnect.

This was impossible. I had to tell her the whole truth, tell her who I really was. I had to make her understand.

"Evangeline, I'm sorry. When I met you, I really did just want to help you. From the first moment, you were different than all the rest, different than any Host or Earthbound I'd ever met. You saw me, saw me as more than who I inhabited."

Strangely, it was at this moment that I couldn't look at her anymore, so I stared at my hands. Adam's hands. Jason's hands. My hands.

"I've gotten to know you, probably better than I've ever bothered to know anyone here," I said. I felt dizzy, desperate. "None of this is your fault, Evangeline. You're a good person. You don't deserve any of this, what Constantine's life, what his choices have brought on you."

I could feel the clock ticking forward, the rush of the god Police's impending arrival.

"But things got out of hand, and I stayed longer than I should have. I made things worse for you." Now I did meet her gaze.

"I should have known when the god Police came that they wouldn't stop until they retrieved me." It felt like I was explaining it to myself as much as to her. "I thought that by killing Adam, I could hide from them. It was selfish and wrong, and in the end, solved nothing. I never thought they'd find me by tracing you."

Her eyes had grown as wide as two moons, and I saw my own face reflected in their depths. I love her, I thought. This is it.

"I never meant to endanger anyone," I pleaded. "I just wanted to help. To help you."

As soon as those last words left my lips, I realized how little sense anything I'd said would make to an Earthbound. Evangeline just stared.

My borrowed heart raced, and I felt a wave of nausea. What had I done? Somehow, I had to make her leave.

"You have to run now, Evangeline. Run as far from here as you can. Run away from me; it's your only chance." I could see she was listening, so I poured on.

"You don't deserve to die. Not this young, not at the hands of the god Police. You could still do some good on Earth. I feel it. It can't be your time yet, at least not on my account. I can't be responsible for your soul's eviction from its Host."

As soon as I said it, I knew it to be true. Somehow, Evangeline was like me. All the Earthbounds, they were just like me. They were all living in their Host bodies, just like we gods did.

We were all Visitors.

What were we doing, we gods? Why did we have the ability to take over their Hosts, their homes? What made us more worthy, more entitled? The more hours and days that I spent here beyond a normal Vacation, the more certain I was that this was wrong. I'd never felt so un-god-like.

It was then I knew. Why the Controller had said that Adam had a mark for greatness, a special destiny.

It wasn't just about him; it was about me. God 201. I was going to change the Playground. By telling them. By telling Earthbounds about Possession. I could put an end to all of this. For good.

Then I noticed that Evangeline had taken a step back, away from the bed. She was looking at me as if I'd lost my mind.

"Adam, you're making no sense…"

Before I could press her further, Caden walked in.

"Oh my god, Adam, you're awake. When I got the call from Evangeline and heard about the plane crash, I was so worried. Are you both alright? I'm here to help any way I can."

He approached the bed and sat down on the edge by my feet, then patted my leg stiffly.

Evangeline rushed over to wrap him in a big hug — I swear I saw him flinch. Evangeline didn't seem to notice and only smiled back at him while he nodded.

What? Something was off, out of synch.

Caden looked back toward the hallway. Relieved to escape our conversation, Evangeline began chatting away excitedly to him. His mind, however, was clearly elsewhere.

"What do you think, Caden; can you help?" Evangeline waited for his response.

Caden nodded, then looked toward the door again.

I felt the hairs rise on the back of my neck, and my heart began to race. Everything in me was telling me that Caden was more awkward and jumpy than usual.

"Caden," I said slowly, "do you remember the day we met?"

Caden twitched, then looked despairingly at Evangeline. "He's still confused by the head injury, I take it?"

Before she could respond, I sat up and reached out to grasp his arm firmly.

"Tell me about the day we met," I said. "I interviewed you in an unusual place, surely you remember?"

His face went blank, and I watched as he searched his memory. Searched Caden's memory.

I knew that look. I knew all about that three-second delay to initiate a download.

Shit. He likely already knew I was on to him. Seconds counted now. I had to be careful. Dropping back onto the bed, I forced a sharp chuckle and placed one hand to my forehead.

"Sorry, Caden, I don't know what came over me there. When you walked in, it just reminded me of when I conducted all those interviews while I had the flu. Questioning everyone from my sickbed, on the couch at the back of the Advertising office, do you remember?" I smiled warmly.

He visibly relaxed, sinking back onto the edge of the bed. "Of course, Adam. I wasn't sure I'd get the job." He laughed dryly.

Liar! It had never happened. We'd interviewed in a bar, my sister's jazz lounge, a few blocks from my offices. It was her birthday, and I'd been planning a surprise, so I'd held the last few interviews there.

Evangeline was studying me carefully, her eyes darting to Caden before settling back on my face again. She was too intuitive; her face showed that she sensed my concern. I needed to come up with a plan before she said anything.

Then Evangeline beat me to it.

"Caden, do you think you could go find the nurse, and ask her if Adam could have something to eat? I'm suddenly famished, and I'm sure he is as well. It's been almost a full day since we had any food." She smiled sweetly.

"Ah, sure. Sure. I'll just be a second." He got up and walked out.

As soon as he was gone, she whispered, "What's going on, Adam? Why don't you trust Caden?"

I sat up and swung my legs over the side of the bed.

"Evangeline, we have to run. Now!"

*   *   *

***Investigative Report by god Policeman #807
re Hospital Incident – Primary Officer Action Notes,
Part 1***

Following the plane crash landing, the Controller traced #201's companion Evangeline to a local hospital. All agents were now aware that #201's Host Adam was no longer traceable and that the Controller had switched to using his companion for tracking, although the cause had still not been determined.

By monitoring Evangeline's activities, it was discovered that god #201 had indeed reclaimed Host Adam shortly after landing the plane. The Controller also noted that Evangeline had contacted with the only other Earthbound aware of their plight, Adam's co-worker Caden.

It was decided that another reclaim attempt would be made.

The Controller assigned new officers #808 and #809 to go Earthbound with me as backup. It was determined that I would take Possession of Host Caden upon his arrival at the hospital, while #808 and #809 were to take Possession of two hospital security guards.

I, posing as Caden, was to go up to #201's hospital room, where I was to separate him from Evangeline and terminate his Host and force his return home. The Controller indicated that I must get Adam alone so that he could be reclaimed without further involvement or undue attention by Earthbounds. She was very unhappy with how the entire airplane attempt had transpired.

Upon entering the hospital, #808 and #809 took up positions by the stairwell and elevator exits, in case #201 managed to get away from me and attempt to flee the hospital. I approached a third hospital security guard, then briefly possessed him in order to take his firearm. I then released him after first concealing the weapon within Caden's jacket.

It was during the elevator ride to the hospital room that I determined this approach to be flawed.

Given that the mission to reclaim #201 had already drawn too much Earthbound attention, and the current plan offered the potential for a lobby assassination (which would be witnessed by many Hosts), I felt I needed to ensure that #201 could be reclaimed in the privacy of his hospital room.

So I came up with a better plan. I'd thought of a way to convince #201 to stop running.

He was committed to being with Host Evangeline. She was the reason he'd overstayed his Vacation. She was the reason he'd repeatedly broken the rules of gods Playground. She was the anchor.

In order to get #201 to surrender, to release his Host and return home, the answer was clear.

I would need to terminate Host Evangeline.

(Resumption of #201 narrative)

* * *

SEVEN

So Many Hosts, So Little Time

While she'd clearly decided to ignore most of what I'd told her as the ramblings of a confused, head-injured patient, Evangeline did agree that something was off with Caden and that we couldn't trust him.

She helped me out of bed, and we slipped into the hallway. We managed to make our way to the stairwell at the far end without encountering any hospital staff, then immediately began heading down the stairs.

I didn't really have a plan. I just knew I had to get us out of that hospital. I had no doubt that Caden was one of the god Police and that we were both in danger.

My mind raced, running through all the possible scenarios. Moments ago, I'd thought it safer for us to separate, but now I wasn't so sure.

Did Evangeline know too much? What would the god Police do to her if they managed to reclaim me? If we separated, would they actually leave her alone? I felt angered by the god Policemen's lack of respect for the lives of surrounding Hosts, yet helpless to do anything to change our path. My instinct to warn Earthbounds was even stronger. But first, I needed to get Evangeline to safety.

I needed to focus. Moral outrage was a wasted emotion without action to back it, and I was running out of options. I would focus on the one thing I could achieve, which was getting Evangeline away from the immediate threat. I would buy myself some time to think. Time to plan.

* * *

Investigative Report by god Policeman #808 re Hospital Incident – Secondary Officer Action Notes, lobby, Part 1

First Policeman #807 had gone upstairs as Host Caden. He seemed confident that he could remove #201 from Host Adam without further incident.

#809 and I were waiting at our assigned posts. Then some new Hosts walked in.

I recognized one of them right away as part of the mob men from Host Evangeline's past; prior to going Earthbound for this assignment, I'd reviewed the barkeep's Memory Files concerning the pub shooting in hopes it would help me determine their intentions and prepare me for any further interference (for further details, please see the Investigative Report of #201's first Body Jumping incident).

The mob men arriving in the hospital weren't very discreet. I spotted the weapons strapped to their hips easily beneath their coats. We would need to intervene.

#809 and I approached the three men as they stood talking to the lobby receptionist. They were politely inquiring as to their "dear friend Adam Juri's room, one of the plane crash survivors, our sister Evangeline is with him."

I stepped forward, eyeing the receptionist to indicate that security would take it from here. "Can we perhaps be of assistance?" I touched his arm, then pulled him away from the desk.

He didn't like that and glanced at his two companions. "Just trying to visit our sister and her friend," he said, but he was clearly becoming agitated.

This was an unexpected complication. We could not let the earth men go upstairs for their target Evangeline as this could interfere with #807's retrieval of #201. The mob men would need to be removed from the equation, which meant we would fail in our mission to keep a lower profile.

I pulled my gun, as did #809. "We need to ask you to leave this hospital," I said, knowing he couldn't do that. He had his own mission. Hosts!

Investigative Report by god Policeman #807
re Hospital Incident – Primary Officer Action Notes, Part 2

Upon the Earthbound Evangeline's request for food, I was forced to briefly leave the hospital room, as I couldn't risk arousing her suspicions while there were still other Earthbounds nearby in the hall. I didn't want to draw their attention, so I entered the elevator and rode one floor down.

As soon as possible, I returned for a second attempt. After confirming the hallway was now clear of Earthbounds, I returned to the hospital room. Upon arrival, I discovered that #201 and the Earthbound Evangeline were no longer in the room.

I contacted the Controller, who traced Host Evangeline to the stairwell, descending towards the lobby. I assumed #201 had realized that I had taken Possession of Host Caden and *decided to flee. I returned to the elevator and rode it to the ground floor, where I located the stairwell entrance.*

I noted that #808 and #809 had left their lobby posts and were chatting with the lobby receptionist, but I did not have the time to confer with them. I was focused on confronting #201 and Host Evangeline in the stairwell. I was confident this would be an ideal location to complete my mission.

(Resumption of #201 narrative)

* * *

We rushed down the stairwell as quickly as we could, but I was still lightheaded and kept stumbling. Evangeline did her best to support me, but our pace was moderate at best.

Jason! Jason, please talk to me! I stumbled again as the memory flashed to the surface and my vision blurred, causing me to pause mid-step. Evangeline hesitated with me.

"Adam, are you ok?"

I wanted to speak, but instead sank to the stairs as my world went dark again.

I was taller now, almost a man. Maybe seventeen. Mother was pulling on my arm, begging me to stay. "Jason, he doesn't know what he's doing. Don't leave! I'm sure when...."

"When what? He sobers up?" I felt breathless, and pushed her arm away so I could reach for the door handle once

more. "I'm sorry, mom. I love you, but I don't know why you stay here, why you let him hurt you."

I stood taller then took a deep breath, knowing there was no turning back once I said my piece.

"I'm done. I've saved up enough money; I can take care of myself now."

Anxious to make my escape, an angry heat flushed through every inch of my body, causing the hair on my arms to stand on end.

"I'm not like him," I roared. "I can be something else, something better than this!"

I gasped, shaking my head to clear the unwanted thoughts.

Rising back on my feet, I nodded to Evangeline. "Keep going; we're almost at the bottom."

As I ran out the door, I shouted again. For my mother's benefit or just to tell the wind, I honestly don't know.

"I'll never need someone like you've needed dad!" I was crying now, but with each step away from the house, I felt stronger.

"I'm going to be someone important. Independent. I'll build my own life. I'm stronger than either of you. You'll see!"

Enough! I took a deep breath, carefully stepped onto the final landing. As Evangeline and I began to descend the third set of stairs, we both spotted the lobby level exit door on the floor below at the same moment. We exchanged relieved glances.

Before we could descend these last few steps, however, the doorway opened.

"There you are!"

Caden stepped into the stairwell. He grasped the railing and leaned forward to smile up at us where we'd stopped, frozen three steps above.

"Caden!" Evangeline tried to cover her distress but unconsciously took a step backward, moving up a stair away from us both.

"Adam decided he felt well enough to get some fresh air. I was just taking him out for a walk. Did you get us some food?" Her voice shook.

Host Caden laughed. "No, no. Why bother, since you both know I'm not Caden?" Then he pulled a handgun from beneath his coat.

Once again, my mind raced, but in reaction to the present moment instead of the past. No time for dreaming or memory flashbacks now. I was trapped and in no shape to run.

He'd shoot me now for certain. I was impossible to miss in this narrow stairwell.

I turned to look back at Evangeline. She looked terrified for me. I felt sad.

Then the god Policeman smiled in a way that Caden's face had never smiled before. Hungrily.

"Calm your fears, young lady. This will all be done soon," he whispered with false tenderness. I watched as his fingers twitched on the gun.

"Playtime's over, 201. It's time for you to return home."

Then the god Policeman winked at me through Caden's face before turning the gun towards Evangeline.

*   *   *

Investigative Report by god Policeman #808
re Hospital Incident – Secondary Officer Action Notes,
lobby, Part 2

The Earthbound Mob Hosts were not open to negotiation. They also pulled their guns.

I exchanged glances with #809. We agreed we had no choice. We began shooting.

The following sequence of events was unavoidable. We recognize that a lobby shootout would result in more undesired attention by Earthbounds, perhaps even several Earthbound causalities.

While confident that no real threat to gods Playground resulted because of our actions, we also accept any disciplinary action deemed warranted. We hope our supervisors and the Controller acknowledge that we were only trying to complete our assigned tasks and that we did terminate the mob Hosts successfully, thus preventing their interference with #807's mission.

(Resumption of #201 narrative)

*   *   *

"What are you doing?" I stared in confusion between god Policeman/Caden and Evangeline.

But inside, I knew. I knew what he'd realized.

"No more games, 201. You've overstayed your Vacation. You've become inappropriately attached to this Earthbound." His finger twitched on the gun's trigger again.

How to save her, how to solve this unsolvable puzzle?

It was at this moment that I experienced a sense of deja vu. While my view of the current situation was in sharp contrast to my perspective at the onset of this Vacation, in a weird convolution of events, my experience of time once again slowed. Although not so pleasurably this time.

I watched with unsuppressed horror as his finger completed its compression and the bullet left the gun. I tracked its path as it travelled like a floating tear across the stark stairwell towards Evangeline's chest.

My gaze locked with Evangeline's. She'd also registered the gunshot, and her eyes had begun to widen with shock. Oh, there it was, that instant when an Earthbound recognizes their own impending demise! Yet so different from any time I'd born witness to it before.

So, I did the only thing I could do.

I Body Jumped.

I guess, foolishly, I thought that somehow I could stop the sequence of events. I could turn back time, control the outcome. I would somehow save her.

Leaving Adam's gift behind, I entered my new Host.

Remarkable! Not at all what I expected!

* * *

Investigative Report by god Policeman #807
re Hospital Incident – Primary Officer Action Notes,
Part 3, conclusion

I heard shots ring out in the lobby behind me through the door. There was no time to investigate.

I shot the Earthbound Host Evangeline as planned. She was only a few feet away, I couldn't miss.

In that last moment, her face seemed to change. Her eyes rolled back, and she began to crumble to the floor. This was before my bullet reached her chest, but still, it found its mark, albeit a bit higher up than I'd intended.

At the same time, I noted that 201's Host Adam had also fallen to the steps below. Had I somehow fired twice?

Placing the gun back in my pocket, I approached their two crumpled bodies.

(Resumption of #201 narrative)

* * *

Even though this was my second experience with this affront of the body, I couldn't help but be surprised by the sensation of the bullet entering the flesh. This time, however, I was more invested, so perhaps that is why it had lost its gentle lover's touch.

Our body recoiled into itself as the bullet ripped apart our flesh. There it was again, that searing bright pain, that blinding, all-consuming, undeniable glory.

We collapsed, and I sighed with resignation at the jolt of our back hitting the cement stair.

I was overwhelmed with guilt. I'd failed her.

Still, I tried to keep us Earthbound. I felt like I could. *Gods didn't die.*

I thought if I could just hold on, I could keep us alert and present until help arrived. Until someone came to revive and repair her body.

But Evangeline had other ideas, apparently.

I felt her rise, the pull of her essence heading upward. Then the extraordinary brightness began to burst, leaving nothing but darkness.

Stay with me!

I let her body heave one last long, disappointed sigh, then let go as well. There was nothing to keep me Earthbound any longer.

Eight

Who's Hosting?

I sighed again, then flowed through the valley of blooms to check in with the Master Controller.

I'd failed in my assignment. What if I wasn't allowed to fix it?

"Ah, the fallen angel returns, I see." The Controller smiled softly at her own joke, but her tone was sympathetic.

"Don't look so defeated. We all knew it probably wouldn't work, regardless of your efforts or sacrifice." She patted my arm.

"The proof is in the pudding; fifty years is enough time. They can't be turned. It was a nice idea, your Vacation experiment. But there really isn't a cure. Surely now you realize that."

No, I couldn't accept that. "Let me try again!" I was pleading, but I didn't care. "I need to go back. We need to go back. I know I haven't filed a report in weeks, so you don't know it all, but it was working this time. I saw a change in...."

The Controller didn't let me finish. She raised her hand dismissively.

"While I appreciate your optimism and desire to save souls, that really isn't for either of us to decide. You knew all along that this experimental idea of yours was just that, an experiment."

She turned back to her station, waving at the charts and logs.

"It was the same result for all of your Higher Agents. All of those souls your group tried to save; they are all still the same selfish, self-focused beings they were before you gave them this second chance."

Turning back toward me, she gave me a sympathetic half-smile. "As we saw, Jason was no different. Just like all the rest, it didn't work. You didn't change him." Her lips pursed, then she said the words I feared most. "You need to shut the Playground down."

"No, wait! He was changing, I saw it. I demand to speak to Nipin first. Tell her I just need more time. It will work. She needs to send us both back. She promised if I could save just one…." I paused, then decided to add some insurance.

"She owes me that much."

The Controller frowned, then gave up a nod. "Fair enough. I'll let her know your request. We won't shut it down just yet."

As I turned to take a seat, the gate opened again behind me.

I watched as they brought him through, being careful to avoid his eyes.

(Resumption of #201 narrative)

* * *

They'd brought me back home. I guess I always knew they would, eventually. I progressed along beside my guard through the clustered lights, down the path my kind knew all too well.

No Vacation Satisfaction Report this time. I was in big trouble. The lost wager was the least of my worries now. I wondered if they knew what I'd decided. If they'd realized that I'd planned to warn Earthbounds. To put an end to the Playground for good.

The Policeman and I reached the check-in counter. "He's all yours," he said, handing the Controller his log. "He'll need to be forced to record a full recount of his Vacation. Multiple breaches, a lot to review. I'll add additional logs if needed once I compare notes with my team. The trial won't occur until after his full recount is recorded."

I ignored the rest of their exchange. It held no interest for me. Nothing mattered now. I glanced wearily about. Even back in my god-like form, I felt exhausted. I'd failed Earthbounds. Failed Evangeline. Failed myself. What if I never got another chance to go back, to do what needed to be done?

Then I noticed a female god sitting in the corner. Waiting for her next Host assignment to go Earthbound, I guess.

Strange I'd been brought through the same Controller. I'd thought they'd keep renegades like myself separate, if for no other reason than the fear we'd talk about what we'd done, about the silliness of the rules we'd broken.

Fear that I might talk about being one of them. About being human. About how I started to care. About the need to stop the Playground.

I turned away and closed my eyes. My mind, however, wouldn't let her huddled image be ignored. Something about her pulled me back, and I reopened my eyes to turn towards her once again.

Now my mind was really playing tricks on me.

Up here, we gods can take any form we wish. *Only us gods here, nothing to see, nothing not to be.* I had changed appearances so often myself I'd lost track of where I'd started. How strange, though….

Her head was down, as though deep in thought. Then she ran her fingers through her flowing hair.

I inhaled sharply, causing both the departing Policeman and the Controller to look back at me in surprise. I had to ask.

"Evangeline?"

Watch for Book 2, the continuation of the gods Playground story, coming soon.
"Only gods Get 2nd Chances"

ACKNOWLEDGEMENTS & DEDICATION

This book would not exist without the encouragement of my family. First, to my dear Honeybee, my inspiration and gift from above, my sweet daughter Melissa. Second to my sweetest prince, my second heart, my son Michael. Finally, to the 'dream big' voice inside my head, the one always pushing me further, my husband Peter.

The final version of this manuscript would not have grown to its full potential without the feedback and encouragement of my wonderful editor, Franny Billingsley. Thank you for pushing me to create the best story I had in me! Thank you also to my friends and group of galley readers, who's additional feedback and notes helped me feel ready to release my latest story for others to see.

Finally, thank you to all the fans, young and old, of my first debut novel, *Habitan*. Your emails, letters, posts, and reviews were an unexpected gift. Your words of enthusiasm and excitement for my secret imagination have helped keep me on the path, and have encouraged me to continue to pursue my story-telling dream. I promise I won't let you down; I will continue writing, for I know you are out there, waiting. Thank you, friends.

I dedicated *Habitan,* a YA fantasy novel about personal strength and faith, to my children. I wrote it in hopes of reminding them of the power of choosing to do the right thing, even when all hope seems lost. Well, here we are again. Like *Habitan*, I hope the underlying message readers find beneath the action in *gods Playground* is that we all have a choice in who we are, and who we can become. We all share the opportunity to do good in this world. Or not. You just need to see beyond yourself, and decide.

So I dedicate this story to those who don't believe in excuses to "go dark." Those who have learned the gift of empathy and reflected joy. May you keep pursing life with kindness, compassion, and a sense of humor, for I believe it is these strengths that help carry us all through the unavoidable misadventures of life, and then, hopefully, allow us one day to depart in peace.

I hope you enjoyed the trip, as I wrote this for you. Until next time. Cheers.